"Here's what I want."

Bolan asked Brognola for two squads of blacksuits, massive air firepower to pave the way for ground troops, and a U.S. aircraft carrier if possible and on the way.

He needed the package put together ten minutes ago. Bolan and company planned to go in and raze the jungle outpost first. He figured a day or two to hammer it down in Papua New Guinea, and by then the colonel's sub would have surfaced in port.

He was going to use the enemy's own base of operations as a launching point to go into North Korea.

Forget political fallout and the DMZ, it was time to strike back.

MACK BOLAN ®
The Executioner

DON PENDLETON'S
THE EXECUTIONER®
ARMAGEDDON EXIT

THE
DOOMSDAY
TRILOGY
BOOK III

A GOLD EAGLE BOOK FROM
WORLDWIDE®

TORONTO • NEW YORK • LONDON
AMSTERDAM • PARIS • SYDNEY • HAMBURG
STOCKHOLM • ATHENS • TOKYO • MILAN
MADRID • WARSAW • BUDAPEST • AUCKLAND

First edition September 2002
ISBN 0-373-64286-5

Special thanks and acknowledgment to
Dan Schmidt for his contribution to this work.

ARMAGEDDON EXIT

We have just enough religion to make us hate,
but not enough to make us love.

—Jonathan Swift

We need to teach our children, and ourselves,
religious tolerance. Hatred of religions we don't
understand make us weak. Knowledge is the
ultimate power.

—Mack Bolan

THE
MACK BOLAN®
LEGEND

Nothing less than a war could have fashioned the destiny of the man called Mack Bolan. Bolan earned the Executioner title in the jungle hell of Vietnam.

But this soldier also wore another name—Sergeant Mercy. He was so tagged because of the compassion he showed to wounded comrades-in-arms and Vietnamese civilians.

Mack Bolan's second tour of duty ended prematurely when he was given emergency leave to return home and bury his family, victims of the Mob. Then he declared a one-man war against the Mafia.

He confronted the Families head-on from coast to coast, and soon a hope of victory began to appear. But Bolan had broken society's every rule. That same society started gunning for this elusive warrior—to no avail.

So Bolan was offered amnesty to work within the system against terrorism. This time, as an employee of Uncle Sam, Bolan became Colonel John Phoenix. With a command center at Stony Man Farm in Virginia, he and his new allies—Able Team and Phoenix Force—waged relentless war on a new adversary: the KGB.

But when his one true love, April Rose, died at the hands of the Soviet terror machine, Bolan severed all ties with Establishment authority.

Now, after a lengthy lone-wolf struggle and much soul-searching, the Executioner has agreed to enter an "arm's-length" alliance with his government once more, reserving the right to pursue personal missions in his Everlasting War.

1

Colonel Bok Chongjin took the radio detonator box as soon as his parachute opened. The way in which he had jumped, twisting as he flew off the GlobeSpecter spy plane's ramp, presented him with front-row viewing of yet another moment of triumph.

Perhaps his biggest victory, and joy, to date.

Jerked skyward, he began his float toward the Pacific. Falling from at least a thousand feet up, he figured he had time enough to enjoy the destruction, allowing the behemoth blackbird to sail a good half mile or so, nose down as it dropped for the water.

Then he hit the button.

It blew better than even Chongjin anticipated. Starting at Nellis—where the prototype superspy-VIP plane was hijacked by the Phoenix Council—Chongjin, his people and their prized Strategic Defense Initiative cargo flew from New Mexico to more than halfway across the Pacific for this DZ, and he knew the wings were still swimming with plenty of fuel for the extra wallop. And, of course, the big bang was launched by several hundred pounds of plastique spread from flight deck to loading bay, all wired to one signal. The spectacle, he decided, was worth both the wait and every dollar of the billions the Americans had invested in the classified superbird. Something sweet, indeed, to be said when he could trample the dreams of others and annihilate their work of genius. Chongjin imagined all the wailing and gnashing of teeth at the hallowed Pentagon, accusations and blame flying all around, more than a few careers all but down the toilet.

The GlobeSpecter nearly slammed to water, a vision of doomsday on the high seas. It was a beautiful sight to behold, Chongjin thought, and laughed. The massive bird came apart in one thundering instant, fireballs meshing next from all points to ignite fuel in the wings. Where the distant horizon joined blue sky and dark water the firestorm boiled into a blazing sheet, fanning out into one giant, roaring demon. Chongjin was forced to squint, keeping an eye on the rising ocean below, but taking in the inferno. He briefly recalled the words of the pilot he'd shot and left on board. Major Temple had been right about one thing—if Chongjin couldn't have the GlobeSpecter, nobody would. Of course, the North Korean colonel could have chanced it, flying it to his homeland, but he couldn't resist scrapping the one-of-a-kind superbird, that middle-finger salute to America Temple had mentioned.

Quite the show, and Chongjin felt momentarily disappointed he couldn't conjure up an encore.

The colonel finagled the steering lines of his parachute, bracing himself for the plunge through the surface, ready to draw in the last breath before going under. Oriented to the surface now, he was getting himself in position to check on who had made it or who was on the verge of drowning, when he spotted the bridge of the nuclear-powered submarine. The hull of the *Kim Jong Il* sliced like some great leviathan across the surface, maybe two miles and closing from the northwest.

Pickup.

Chongjin quickly took in the drop zone. They started splashing through the surface at a stagger, according to wind drift and who had jumped first.

Now the tough part, he knew. He set his sights on the only few canopies he cared about. More than a few of the American hostages were destined to be left behind for the ocean and the sharks to dispose of.

JOHN WALLACE WAS far more relieved when the canopy opened than he had been after the bloody success of taking down the GlobeSpecter at Nellis Air Range.

Only this particular nightmare task had just begun.

East, where the first group had jumped, he saw ten or more spumes rising from the ocean's surface, much higher than the ones harnessed to canopies when they hit water. Whether those poor bastards had frozen in midfall or their canopies failed to open, thanks to intentional sloppy rigging, a lot of folks were now fish food. The bodies bobbing in the water might as well, he thought, have bounced off concrete. A few others, he knew, would drown, tangled in the steering lines or swallowing water as they shot to the surface, too damn scared to time it right when they broke to go under, choking out right beneath their canopies. Mass panic on the DZ was seconds away, the ocean poised to claim more victims. With a few possible exceptions, they were all civilians, SDI brainiacs, he knew, with no military background, not even an amateur sky diver among the lot, if he judged the faces and voices raised in alarm right before they went off the ramp. Factor in the crosswinds and currents on this impossibly vast stretch of the Pacific, the entire group—survivors—would drift far apart before any pickup. It was a disaster, no question, the crazy colonel having known the doomsday score all along. Unless he missed his guess, Wallace guessed Chongjin was thinning out the herd, shaving off the fat now he figured they were relatively safe over international waters.

The waves, of course, didn't look like much from a thousand feet up, but the tide would carry them wherever it wanted, since Mother Nature didn't care about the plans of all her little people. A few them had even cried they couldn't swim. And the only life preserver was the nuke-powered sub, coasting now, he observed, across the surface, still a couple of miles or so to the north, the monster steel fish angled to come in alongside.

The explosion sounded nearly on top of him. He worked the steering line, twisting. The blast did just what the crazy colonel wanted.

In fact, to his sudden horror and concern, it did far more.

Wallace watched the wreckage winging out, spewing hunks his way. Geysers were touched off across the surface of the ocean as debris rocketed away in all directions. And then he cursed Chongjin as the mastermind behind this insane part of the mission.

A jolting look to the side, and he saw the metallic disk, propelled by all the fuel roaring into a fire cloud the size of a battleship, was flying straight on a collision course for his drop. It was as if the damn thing were a magnet or a compass, locked in, going for the intercept to slice him in half right in his harness. Furious, Wallace struggled with the buckle, gripping and pulling and cursing. It came free and he was out of the straps, dropping as he heard the razoring tear of the canopy. A close shave, but he was free-falling, head still on his shoulder, thirty or so feet from touchdown. Even before he hit, sucking in a deep breath, he was curious, and more than a little nervous about who the colonel would deem worthy enough for pickup.

THE PORN THUGS WISHED to go out with a roar.

Mack Bolan didn't have a problem obliging them. No mercy, no prisoners.

No sweat.

The man known as the Executioner nailed the first one just as the North Korean thug came running around the corner of the locker row, a machine-pistol up and tracking. A 3-round burst stitching up the chest, and the hardman was jitterbugging back, crashing through the lockers. The prop was made of cardboard and half of the row came down on top of the corpse in crushed matchsticks. While the soldier's team of backup agents peeled off to link up with agents down the far end of the last row of lockers, Bolan attempted to drive the shooters his way. He zeroed in on the shouting, his M-16 up and searching. He was rounding the corner when another hardman was snatching a naked Asian porn starlet by the hair. He was hauling up his human shield when he spied the big man in black rolling his way. He almost had himself covered with the starlet, the compact Ingram on the way to press itself against her temple, when the Executioner unloaded another short burst. The rounds obliterated the hardman's features to crimson jelly, the woman dropping and crawling away before the body even toppled.

That left two, at least in the immediate vicinity, and Bolan was charging on. He had them sighted in the next second. The two hardmen were torn between the soldier and the Omega agents, shuffling now out of the hole in a shower stall, ready to beat a fighting exit. The Executioner held back on the trigger, zipping them left to right until he burned out the clip. They hit the deck in tandem, blood pooling for the drain.

Bolan thumbed on his tac radio. "Hold your fire! I'm coming out!"

One of the agents copied, and the Executioner moved out in the area between the lockers and the shower. They were fielding sitreps across the board, all units confirming they were still scouring the complex for hostiles. He couldn't be positive, but Bolan weighed the abrupt end of weapons fire all around. Unless the good guys got lucky, there would be no prisoners to grill, no wealth of intelligence to unearth that would further clue the warrior in to the enemy's scheme. Just as well, Bolan decided. It was time to take them down, porn goons or the vipers at the top, wherever and whenever he could root them out.

It was a wrap there, he sensed, nothing to do now but zip up the bodies.

Aloha Productions was shut down. Next on his list was its owner—Colonel Bok Chongjin.

THOMAS SHAW WASN'T the praying sort. Most of his adult life he had always trusted in his own intellect, his talent in demand by NASA and various intelligence agencies as the premier scientist in the ballistic missile and SDI field carrying him through any tough times. Which were few and far between over the years, as the family man led a quiet, comfortable and sedentary life. All of that, life in a bubble, felt like a thousand years ago, another world, another man he'd only dreamed about.

Somehow he was different, but he wasn't sure how or much less if he liked the change.

Since the kidnapping, the internal evolution was slow and gradual, but once started it was a seething cauldron of emotion wanting to carry him away.

Rage. Hope. Terror. Vengeance.

The words never actually took on anything he could call solid mantras for deliverance, but short bursts imploring help from above, to at least keep his wife and daughter alive and safe, shot in and out of his thoughts.

Trench prayers, he believed they were called. It was all beyond his control. There seemed nowhere to turn, nothing else that would—or could—help. Just after the nightmare had begun for himself and his wife and daughter, he found he was indeed praying more often to a universal deity he hadn't thought about in decades. Right then he prayed their canopies opened as soon as Rebecca and Patti jumped—and they did. It was, he knew as he watched them floating toward the dark mass of water some eight or nine hundred feet below, just the beginning of the danger. From there on it would take action, not hoping or wishing for someone or some divine force to come through and lend a helping hand. The madman had told them all to get themselves oriented to the surface as soon as they jumped, time their plunge and draw in a deep breath before they hit. After that they were to unlatch the harness and swim away from their point of insertion so they wouldn't get smothered by the canopy and drown. All of it sounded logical enough, but...

Shaw watched them dropping, fluttering about in the wind draft. He somehow stayed on line—an act of God?—then the massive explosion jarred him to a new height of terror. The scientist knew he had to act as soon as he hit water. Forget the feeling of utter horror and despair that wanted to paralyze him. Forget the superplane that was being obliterated all over the ocean, the roar of the blast sounding nearly on top of his canopy. He reckoned, if nothing else, he should be grateful their captors hadn't bothered feeding them since the abduction or when the canopy had opened to violently jerk him back for the sky he might have soiled himself. Small comfort, even a stupid thought under these dire circumstances, but his mind seemed to pick and choose the strangest areas for whatever relief, whatever dignity he could salvage in the face of a madness he wouldn't have witnessed in some fever-induced nightmare.

He saw his family vanish beneath the surface, heart lurching at the sight, but he believed he would hit roughly twenty to thirty feet beyond them, if he judged the wind drift correctly. They would both need his help—there was nobody else since everybody was on his or her own, splashing around and yelling now—and he looked inside, searching, asking for a strength to do something he wasn't sure he could.

The foamy whitecaps seemed to boil harder and faster as he got closer. He sucked in a deep breath, held it, then closed his eyes against the slash of salt water. He plunged through the surface and was jolted instantly by the cold envelopment of the Pacific.

He lurched up, aware his canopy was ballooning with water, and unsnapped the harness, surprised for a second at his own speed and reaction. He wasn't a sky diver by any stretch, nor much of a swimmer. He was nearly as afraid of water as heights. Somehow instinct for survival, though, propelled by sheer panic to save his family, took over, possessing him to find his wife and daughter or exhaust himself to drowning in the attempt. He scissored his arms and legs, heard thrashing everywhere. Stroking for the surface, he made out shadows in all directions, murky distortions of human shapes framed by fractured shafts of sunlight in the hazy cauldron of ocean. He shoved away the more terrifying thoughts and images of predators now on the move, alerted and excited by all the commotion, then primal senses like radar locked onto the noise and fear, eager for easy meals.

His head broke the surface. Gasping for air, Shaw started stroking with even more fury and energy in the direction he'd seen them go under. Everywhere there were cries for help, a whirlwind of panic-stricken voices, some close, some far. There were gurgling noises as if a number of the abductees were already drowning, their pleas so loud and horrifying it could have been a microcosm of the human race screaming for salvation as the world was about to end in some unholy conflagration.

"Becky! Patti!"

He slammed through a wave, eyes stung by the salt water, gagging on bitter fluids, but calling their names even as another wave slapped him in the face. Stroking on, he nearly bowled through her, but somehow recognized his daughter's face in the stinging blur. She was choking, pounding at the water. Another voice, close now, soothing somehow in its tone of calm command as Shaw reached out for his daughter.

"I have you, Mrs. Shaw! Relax your body, scissor your legs. Our boat is here! You will be safe!"

It was one of the colonel's men, Shaw found, his head barely visible above the water as he kept his arm locked around Rebecca's waist.

"Patti, it's dad! Give me your hand!"

He pulled her close, fighting to stay afloat, legs scissoring, but he felt the limbs growing heavy, weary. Then his daughter cried out at the sight of something over his shoulder. Voices were yelling from behind, urging for action. Shaw turned, puzzled and afraid when his daughter let go and swam past. The man was struggling to haul his wife past him, too, Shaw stroking around when he saw what at first he thought was some great, dark whale. The furious shouting above and beyond, the long poles being dropped in the water, and Shaw realized the leviathan from the deep was their submarine pickup.

WALLACE SIMPLY WANTED to make the sub, hit the deck, take five and have a cigarette.

Son of a bitch! Somehow the pack of smokes had been torn from the waterproof Velcro-fastened pouch of his blacksuit. He'd have to bum one off one of the Korean submariners. Right then he knew he had a bigger problem to solve than a nicotine fit.

On the hard swim to the hull he did something he briefly found out of character, being a black-ops killer who had grown to have no regard for human life. Chalk it up to reflex more than anything else, although he did hear a small voice in the back of his head mention something about a little bonus for his loyalty and concern for the crazy colonel's SDI trophies.

So he hauled in the genius and his wife, maybe fifteen feet from the hull, barking in their ear to swim. Some cursing to keep them motivated, practically holding them up, he shoved them ahead while he fought to keep from going under. Bobbing, he spotted the North Korean submariners on the deck. They were extending poles with hooks on the end, hauling a few of the thrashing crowd out of the water, sliding them up the hull for the deck like nets of fish. About ten of the waiting sub-mariners up there were toting the North Korean version of the AKM assault rifle, looking itchy to cut loose.

"Grab the goddamn cleats and haul your sissy geek asses up the side!"

Enough of the nice-guy routine, Wallace increased the cussing and the shoving a notch when he sensed them floundering some more. The wife managed on her own, squalling just the same, but grabbed hold of the cleat just as the ladder threatened to coast by. She took a second to look back and cursed him like a drunken sailor—man, she had some guts, and a nice ass—but Wallace was too involved wrangling the hubby ahead, lacing the lifeguard routine with vicious shoves and curses, finally throwing him at the lowest cleat when the waves bounced him off the hull like a rubber ball. Another shove to the man's rear and he was moving behind the scientist, up the cleats, and landing on the deck none too soon.

Wallace felt chilled to the bone from the water and the unnerving cries of those out there and drifting farther away from the sub. He had a sneaking suspicion what was next, scanning the grim faces lined along the deck, and the colonel wasn't long in disappointing.

Shivering, Wallace just wanted some dry clothes and a cigarette. He was wondering if the colonel would be so kind as to hand over another weapon since he slapped at an empty holster, having lost the pistol during the jump. Wallace was easing down the deck next, when Chongjin started pointing at the swimmers closest to the sub, barking orders in Korean to his men.

It was selective salvation time.

Wallace found his three men from Nellis had made it out of the water and onto the deck, his confidence buoyed some by the fact he was still among his own kind of people. Major Temple had been curiously absent for the jump, nowhere now to be found on deck or in the water. That put Wallace on alert. If Chongjin started weeding out his own players one by one, whether their asking price was too high or for some other reason, it meant no one was invaluable to the council's final goals.

He found the trio of SDI trophies, wives and the girl—now heaving her guts—had passed the survival-of-the-fittest grade, of course, hugging themselves and dancing around near the bridge, shaking like wet dogs. A woman dragged onto the deck next, and that—lo and behold—would be Ms. Miles, the gutsy lady Chongjin had been seconds away from shooting back in New Mexico. He couldn't help but wonder about her real impression on Colonel Compassion, since she wasn't too shabby to look at, breasts nicely molded against her soaking blouse, a rear end that belonged more to an aerobics instructor than a government gal who sat around all day.

Moving on, Wallace noted the charter members—minus Mr. FEMA, of course, who had been shot by Chongjin before they took flight—had made it out of the ocean. The American heads of the Phoenix Council were slapping at dripping water, scowling around. A beefy Korean in a dark pea coat with a dozen or so shining epaulets and bill cap—the submarine's commander,

Wallace assumed—was nodding, grinning at the other Americans doing their damnedest to swim for the hull. He was going back and forth a little with Chongjin in rapid-fire Korean as if it were all some big joke. The sub's commander gestured toward all the GlobeSpecter wreckage, most of it burning, Wallace noted, some hunks still floating down and splashing to the ocean. The commander indulged a belly-ripper laugh at the sight of the destruction.

Freak show, Wallace thought.

Wallace didn't understand the curt order thrown down the deck by Chongjin, but he caught the gist of it. And he could sure as hell read body language. All poles went overboard. The real panic and cries of terror erupted from those destined to be stranded as they figured it out. The submariners cut loose with a volley of autofire.

Then the real drama, Wallace watched, unfolded on the deck. Shaw went berserk, charging one of the shooters. His wife was screaming his name, the colonel roaring now as the SDI scientist nearly bowled one of the shooters overboard. For a second Wallace was sure the other Koreans were going to turn their weapons on the man, but Chongjin stepped in between Shaw and his executioners.

"You can't do this! You can't just kill them or leave them behind!"

"Go below, Mr. Shaw! Now! Need I remind you I saved the lives of your loved ones? Take them below before I change my mind!"

The shooting stopped. The commander was still grinning from the bridge, relaying orders down the hatch as the "saved" were escorted up the ladderway by armed guards.

They were still wailing in the waves, he saw, but the killing stopped. Must have been a message, get the hell away from my sub, Wallace figured. Five bullet-riddled bodies, he tallied, floated away, a few wounded groaners going under. And all that blood was now spreading.

The sharks would come soon enough, no mistake. Some bigger, some more aggressive than the rest.

The merc fell in with the rest of the survivors. Chongjin was checking faces, and when Wallace found the colonel getting to him he would have sworn the crazy North Korean was disappointed Wallace had made the deck. Screw him, he thought, then growled at the closest submariner for a smoke.

2

"They blew the plane, Striker. Right after—get this—they jumped for the Pacific. Bad guys *and* hostages."

"Where?"

"According to Stony Man Farm's scoping of the AIQ, almost four hundred miles northwest of Hawaii, Kauai to be exact. They were picked up by a sub, the *Kim Jong Il.*"

Bolan drew a mental map of the area, the cell phone with secured line to Hal Brognola pressed to his ear. "That would put the colonel and company maybe more than halfway home to Pyongyang by now. And I bet you're going to tell me that sub isn't diesel-electric driven."

"You'd win the bet, but it gets a damn sight worse than dealing with the only nuclear-powered submarine we're aware the North Koreans have. I neglected a few details."

The heavy pause on the other end didn't inspire Bolan with confidence. While the director of Sensitive Operations brought on more bad news, Bolan gave the secured perimeter of the porn studio's lot a scoping. Justice Department and FBI agents had Aloha Productions under control, the lot swarming with a conveyor belt of various law-enforcement officers, in and out of the studio, most still sweeping the inner hive for lurking gunmen or employees in hiding. There were pockets across the lot where studio employees were being grilled by agents, almost all of whom stonewalled so the pat story of the hour was that they didn't have a clue and were simply hired as adult film stars.

A good ninety minutes had been chewed up with a final walk-through, but no more North Korean gunmen turned up. Surrounding streets were cordoned off by whatever LAPD units could be spared since jihad had finally erupted in the city. Sitreps were in from law enforcement around town, and there was some good news on at least that one front against the terrorists. Nine out of the thirteen Iraqi jihad troops had been burned down with little more than collateral damage to downtown buildings. No civilian or police casualties, other than some dings and scrapes when two human bombs went off before the jihad soldiers were taken out by SWAT snipers. That left four on the loose, Bolan knew, but the latest word from the FBI was they had definite sightings of suspicious persons loosely matching descriptions of their late brothers-in-mayhem in the vicinity of Long Beach.

For his part, Bolan had some potential good news to deliver when the head Fed finished filling him in. When the last shooter had dropped, Bolan was fairly positive nothing of intelligence value would turn up. But the Executioner discovered that, even in his world, sometimes being wrong could balance the scales. They weren't tipped in his favor yet, but the office-suite of the late Bu Jin had uncovered what the soldier suspected, and hoped, was a jackpot of cold facts to some questions that had hung over his head about the enemy up to that point. Apparently when the hired hitman, Robert Bowen, had blown away the colonel's front man in Aloha Productions, the body crashing into the wall had opened a section that led to a vault of videotapes. To read the labels, or whatever was on film, Agent Michaels was right then scrounging up what he'd called one of the fine Korean actresses. Dozens of videos stashed away for somebody's eyes-only screening, and Bolan had passed the order to bag them up for later viewing and interpretation by the men at the ultracovert Stony Man Farm.

Taking the update from the big Fed, Bolan felt his anger building toward simmering rage with each grim revelation. Brognola informed him of furor over at the Pentagon about the prototype GlobeSpecter being trashed, with plans hitting the drawing board to sink the sub, only the President hadn't yet given the thumbs-up for any action, covert or otherwise. Coast Guard and Navy fast-lift boats and choppers were in the vicinity of the crash to scoop up survivors. Brognola next put the rescue nightmare point-blank. What had happened was both caught on satellite imagery and witnessed by a fighter squadron out of Hawaii. From the present head count of survivors, it was determined at least half of the abductees had been left stranded in the water while Chongjin's ride submerged and vacated. The ones the colonel deemed unfit to further his agenda were treated to a round of autofire. Not a clean execution sweep, as Chongjin left behind breathing and bleeding meals. With all the blood in the water, an hour or so later the first sharks began showing up.

Brognola fell into a silence that Bolan measured in heartbeats of burning anger.

"Just about everything we have for antisubmarine warfare, from Hawaii to Japan," Brognola said, "has been deployed. The sub is about a hundred meters down, moving at close to forty knots. They're sacrificing quiet for speed. Another gesture of defiance from Chongjin, daring us to blow the ship out of the water. I don't think that's going to happen, no telling what they might have in terms of any medium range cruise-type missiles that could be packed with nukes. With the ASW screen we have blanketing that part of the world, we figure two days or less they'll be docking. We have a good idea where that will be."

"And we just let them pull into port? Walk our people into Pyongyang, victorious conquerors?"

"Believe me, I understand your frustration, and I've burned the Man's ear all I can to get you and a blacksuit team the green light."

"So we just keep cleaning up the mess."

"For now. But the scuttlebutt I'm catching from the Oval Office, and especially since Chongjin decided to use American citizens for shark chum, is that the Man is close to giving a green light for some sort of covert action into North Korea. I'm talking about going in and having Chongjin drawn and quartered if that's what it takes. My feeling is it will be a retaliatory strike, the rumbles I'm catching, and damn the political fallout.

What I hear, President Kim Jong isn't taking any calls from our President. Now the sub angle, it caught everybody off guard. Our own intelligence people blew the call there. Last anybody heard, their spy subs didn't even have adequate sonar setups."

"Makes you wonder."

"Indeed it does. It sure smells like somebody on our side, real high up, has been blowing smoke for a long time. Fact this office wasn't even aware North Korea had a nuke sub...I know, too late now to cry about it."

Bolan wanted to push his role along with Brognola, but the soldier understood the waiting game. "We turned up some tapes here you might want to have some of your people take a look at. I'm thinking Chongjin was keeping his film classics stashed here with a few prominent faces. Extortion bait."

"Get them to me ASAP."

"I guess you've heard the news already."

"The jihad out there? Yeah. Let the troops out that way handle it from there, Striker. I have something else for you that might put us closer to the Man giving us the blessing to go for Chongjin's head if it pans out. I've checked it out through a source of mine I'd bet my pension is one hundred percent reliable, so I need you to look into it. Grimaldi is on the way to Edwards Air Force Base, but I don't want you to wait around for him."

"Let's have it."

STEPHEN TOLLEY WAS finished running. They were coming. It was just a question of when and how many they would send. When they did show up, it wouldn't be to extend any olive branch, try to bring him back into the fold, all's forgiven. He would be ready when they came for his scalp, a show of force on his part that would answer any and all of their questions as to why he'd stabbed them in the back. In fact, he was already prepared to dish them back the same taste of hell they'd brought to America.

It was the waiting game that was eating on his nerves, but he figured he'd endured this long—eight months on the run and hiding—so what did difference did another hour or two make?

Still, the paranoia was getting to him, making him see and hear things that weren't there. Or were they? Even in the dead of night the Mojave Desert was alive with its own strange and eerie overtures, its vast emptiness rifling with the frequent coyote howl or the rustle of tumbleweed blown by a sudden wind gust coming down from the hills sounding as if it echoed up from the bottom of a tomb. Every moan and cry could easily mask the sound of a stealthy advance by foot on the ramshackle abode at the base of the Cady Mountains.

A major concern.

He went to the living-room window, HK-33 assault rifle locked and loaded and in hand, the .45-caliber Glock riding in shoulder leather. Depending on the numbers, there was the HK Benelli shotgun canted against the recliner, a riot piece with the potential to blast a couple of them off their feet, hell, saw them in half if he was quick enough on the trigger. Only he didn't intend to see them crash the doors, swarm the room and shoot him down like some cornered animal.

This night he intended to be the one full of unpleasant surprises.

The pressure plates beneath the planks on the front and back landings, just inside the stoops, had been wired to the plastique blocks two days ago, ever since he began making the round of calls to the Justice Department. They were armed now and ready for business. The phone number, the plastic explosives and weapons were retribution gifts left to him by his late comrade in the Defence Intelligence Agency's CCS. The assignment to the DIA's Counter-CounterSurveillance, which was essentially their own spies watching their own spies, was where the nightmare had all begun for him. That was part of the problem, since his own people, traitorous scum they were, knew all the tricks of the trade. The tip-off happened right before he bailed D.C. and made the long run to the Mojave to seek sanctuary with his retired comrade. They hadn't just frozen his bank accounts; they had wiped them out. With only credit cards at his disposal, it was easy enough, he knew, to track him there as he was forced to purchase gas and food with Visa and Mastercard. The secured line on the cell phone wasn't guaranteed, either, since he knew they had state-of-the-art intercepting eavesdropping devices. They could hide in the hills and listen through parabolic mike. The only plus he could factor in was that he was all alone in the world. No wife, no kids, none who knew and cared anymore about his existence.

And the one friend he had in the world was no longer around to aid and assist in what he knew was a coming war in the desert, but he'd known the man's days had been numbered long before arriving. Before Fred Kearnes had finally succumbed to the ravages of brain cancer under that very roof, he had urged Tolley to make the call and sound the alarm on what they both knew was happening across the country, and who was behind it.

And the siege America had come under during the past couple of days was nothing, he knew, compared to what lurked in the wings.

A long scoping of the desert, tumbleweed rolling down the dirt trail, his eyes wanting him to believe every dancing shadow created by a cloud scudding beneath the moon was a gunman on the move. he went back to the surveillance cameras, another gift left behind to help turn the shack into a minifortress. The soft glow of the monitors competed with the light radiating from the television set, more flickering shadows that further tweaked his nerves. The sound muted from the TV, the silence inside and out the shack seemed to amplify with desert noise. Nothing on the screens, the four-eyed minicam atop the roof able to monitor the sweeping desolation through infrared probing on all points. Nothing on the motion sensors. He'd seen them, two days now, riding around the desert in their black GMCs, right after he'd placed the first call to Justice. Sometimes they'd ride on, while other times a man would get out of the vehicle, lift the binoculars to his eyes and malinger in the broiling sun. Hell, they did everything but wave—or blow him off the desert with one well-placed rocket. Making him wait and worry was part of their strategy. This night, though, he could feel them, out in the desert, closing.

Coming soon.

He went to the kitchen window, jumping some at the sound of his own feet creaking over the bare wood floor. He pulled back the curtain, staring at the darkness and at the black hills. His SUV was parked a good fifty yards off to the east, far enough to escape immediate collateral damage when ground zero blew. If he even made it that far.

He was told one man was on the way to save his bacon. Someone named Mike Belasko from the Justice Department. A man he had never laid eyes on but was solemnly assured he could trust with his life.

Tolley was prepared to do just that. Only where was he? The hours had dragged, this one-man savior supposed to have already been in the neighborhood so Tolley could hand off the disks of the who's who and what's what on the Phoenix Council. Belasko was on his way up from L.A. The directions were clear enough, if Belasko marked off the mileage from Barstow to the trio of trailer homes isolated off I-15 coming east and didn't blow past the Joshua tree. But if they had been listening maybe his savior had been ambushed. Maybe that was why they hadn't come storming the shack yet, holding back, sharpening their blades to cut the throat of any cavalry he called in.

Hope and hold on. It was all he could do. A moment's look at the dirt mound where he'd buried Kearnes at his friend's insistence, and he told himself at least he was still alive. A man had a lot of time, he considered, to think and worry when he was all by his lonesome in the middle of godforsaken desolation, the only soul for miles around in the belly of the devil. And to think his friend had lived out there, a desert rat, more or less shutting himself off from the world, waiting to die, shot a wave of hot pain through Tolley's chest. Well, he'd known Kearnes for years, the Batman and Robin of Spookdom. His late friend had proved himself a stand-up act of integrity over the years, and he'd staked his life coming there, revealing something that his buddy wasn't all that surprised to hear. Tolley was a lot like Kearnes, he decided in a moment of sorrow and regret. The job had consumed his life, cost him a couple marriages and children he hadn't spoken to in years. It was lonely as hell out there, but that was the way Kearnes wanted it. It seemed he had just tired of the world, too old, too jaded, had seen too much, viewing his own fate as perhaps a blessing. It might have been the fact he was simply standing at death's door, filling his last days with some wistful remembering, looking back at life with a fair amount of regret and heartache, killing the pain with booze, talking in a solemn, philosophical way about the sorry state of the world. Life's a trade-off. The good guys rarely win one.

He heard the low rumble, sounding from the west. His heart felt like some runaway train about to derail as he raced back for the front window.

One look at the line of big GMCs slowly rolling down the trail, still a mile or so out, and he began counting them off. Six vehicles altogether, so that would make...

Son of a bitch. Twenty to twenty-five men coming to his door.

A small army.

He almost laughed out loud, aware that even if his one-man savior from the Justice Department made the scene they were facing odds so long not even a degenerate gambler would place a bet.

Tolley couldn't wait on any angels of deliverance. He turned from the window to make the final preparations.

THE JOSHUA TREE reared up suddenly out of the dark, and if Bolan hadn't been clocking the miles since Barstow, then the three trailer homes, he would have missed the trail.

Swinging off the highway, the Executioner eased off the gas and guided the Crown Victoria down the hard-packed earth, jouncing some in his seat as he navigated around the deeper ruts. He would have preferred a chopper ferry, but with the situation still hot and uncertain back in Los Angeles, no winged rides could be spared. He could have insisted, using his own authority to command a chopper, but the soldier wasn't about to give the enemy any edge by removing a single bird from the skies over L.A. One more terrorist had gone down in West Hollywood, no twisted glory for that jihad man as he failed to ignite himself when a SWAT sniper took him out from a chopper. That left three, and the Executioner knew all hands would be needed back there. But if Brognola had pulled him off the hunt...well, the Executioner had known his friend long enough to know he wasn't being sent on some wild-goose chase.

The drive gave him time to think, once he finally made it far enough up I-15, stuck in traffic for an agonizing stretch as panicked citizens fled the killing ground of Los Angeles proper.

He didn't know much about Stephen Tolley other than he was a DIA spook with information he'd compiled about the Phoenix Council's operations and future agenda. According to Brognola he'd fled D.C., armed with the goods on the heads of the men Bolan wanted. Whether the soldier was simply being marched into a trap, the whole handing off of intel an elaborate ruse to isolate him in the Mojave Desert...

He would know, two miles and counting.

At that point, Bolan would take anything the man had on Chongjin and his cutthroat horde.

The soldier felt his combat instincts ignite as he scanned the scrub-and-boulder-studded country, the rolling jagged ridges of black hills. There was a familiar itch at the base of his neck, warning him he was either being followed or watched. The M-16/M-203 combo rested against the shotgun seat and the war bag was perched within an easy grab. He was in full combat harness now, pouches stuffed with spare clips and an assortment of grenades. The handheld radio was clipped to his belt, and any moment he expected Jack Grimaldi to raise him from the chopper if he was in the neighborhood. If this was indeed an ambush, Grimaldi, he thought, couldn't get there soon enough.

Beyond this shadow rendezvous, Bolan was counting on Brognola to convince the President to give Stony Man the green light to go hunting for Chongjin, even if that meant rolling right into Pyongyang. There were sticky political ramifications, of course, Bolan suggesting they use any number of U.S. bases in South Korea as a launch point across the DMZ. As always, when it came to dealing with his enemies, the only kind of diplomacy the Executioner intended to put on the table would come from the barrels of his weapons. And as far as the soldier was concerned, it was long gone now for even the most nervous politicos in Washington to care whose toes got stepped on. For one thing, Chongjin couldn't have pulled off the seemingly impossible task of kidnapping American citizens, then hijacking a prototype superplane without inside help. And most likely it would prove the kind of assistance that reached somewhere near the top of the power structure on the home side.

Bolan was committed to taking down any traitor wherever he could root them out even if they were hiding in the White House or the Pentagon. Few things he despised more than a traitor.

He killed the lights and slipped on the night-vision goggles, gauging the mileage to a decent stretch where he could go in on foot and recon.

After parking and shutting off the engine, he hauled out the war bag and bailed. With his M-16 leading the way, the soldier was moving up an incline in the trail when he made out the soft rumbling of an engine.

Several vehicles from the sound of it. Not good. Moments later he discovered he wouldn't need the night-vision goggles after all. He gave the hills a final search for hunkered shadows, his combat radar blipping, and shed the glasses. There was enough light washing over the shack from six GMCs to light up a football field.

The DIA man on the run had told Brognola he feared for his life. As Bolan counted the number of blacksuits disgorging from vehicles, fanning out to encircle the shack, HK MP-5 subguns in hand, he reckoned Tolley wasn't just a raving paranoid.

The Executioner crouched in a narrow gully, assessing his next move. Shadows were marching for the front porch, another team peeling off for the back. That wasn't any welcome-home bunch for Tolley, he knew, and Bolan feared it might turn out to once more be too little too late.

TOLLEY CROUCHED beneath the scissoring fingers of the light show hitting the front of the house. The TV was up to full volume now, a late-night talk show covering any noise he might make on his way out. The nylon satchel with its disks and spare clips around his shoulder, he threw open the section of floor and squeezed down through the hole. There wasn't much crawl space leading out, three feet at its highest point, but it was only a dozen feet to reach the edge of the structure. It was enough.

And then what? Hopefully the blast would take out most of the bastards. Again, what next, if survivors were left standing?

He stretched out on his belly and heard them opening doors, boots hitting the hard earth, marching in some crunching cadence now. As he crabbed ahead on elbows and knees, he had a sudden terrifying vision of snakes under the shack. Yes, he'd checked out the route yesterday, clearing the way of cobwebs and rocks, but he'd heard snakes came out at night, drawn to body heat.

Snakes of the human kind, though, were on the move,

and he saw their shadows breaking through the beams of light around him. Fanning out, just as he hoped, going for the front and back doors.

Three more feet and he was out, then it occurred to him they might know about the crawl space, a shooter waiting for him....

He shoved the fear out of his mind. If they were waiting, prepared to gun him down or simply hold him up for grilling, then as soon as the first pair of feet hit the pressure plates he was gone anyway.

Problems over.

He slithered out from under the edge of the house. Clear in both directions. He jumped up, breaking into a sprint up the short incline. Tolley was leaping and tumbling behind the series of boulders he'd chosen earlier as his point of cover when the earth blew up behind him.

3

John Wallace believed it was easy enough to read the thoughts behind their eyes. No psychic, but he could almost see their anxiety, fear and anger. The situation pretty much spoke for itself, begging any number of questions. Even he wanted to know where it all went from there.

Fat chance, he thought—in all likelihood not even the crazy colonel had any real map for the future.

They were in the wardroom, packed tight around the short conference table, nearly sitting in each other's laps. It was a sub, of course, which meant space was a luxury, but Wallace wasn't about to find a quiet place anytime soon. Sailing along at top speed, Wallace was surprised how much noise the damn thing made. He half expected the whole leviathan to come apart anytime the way it shook, rattled and rolled. Reading deeper into the faces around him, he could be sure the council wished they were somewhere else right then, anyplace other than a couple hundred feet below the surface, aware—as he was—the future was as dark and uncertain as ever.

The remaining four charter members of the Phoenix

Council busied themselves with cigarettes or brandy passed out by Chongjin, as if the indulgence bought them time to gather the courage to fire off a salvo of questions. Naturally the colonel—his sub, his show— had claimed the head of the table and appeared to be collecting his own thoughts for what Wallace knew would be a pep talk, rife with warning and innuendo, even as he reassured them all was well on the next leg of the journey.

Small comfort now, but like the others pulled out of the ocean, Wallace had been issued a blue jumpsuit, much like prisoner coveralls, complete with flip flops. He was dry, calmed down by booze, a cigarette in his fingers, but no gun. Creature comforts, he knew, were the least of anybody's concerns. Being weaponless concerned him now more than ever. Eventually he'd broach the subject with Chongjin.

Jeffrey Hill got the rally started. "Well, Colonel, now what?"

"We stick to the plan."

"Whose plan? And stick to what? So far, you've gotten everything you wanted."

"I hardly see it that way."

Hill was pushing it, even though Wallace could be sure the memory of Chongjin shooting the FEMA man was still fresh in everyone's memory.

"You realize," Henry Jacklin said, "that we can't go back to America now. We've been branded traitors. You left a well-known dead face on the ground back in New Mexico. They'll figure it out. Once we land in your country...need I say it?"

Wallace listened to the long pause, the council not sure which way to proceed with the airing of their fears and worries.

"You will be taken care of once we arrive in my country, gentlemen. I agree there are details to work out, but in due time we will be back on course. I realize certain things have changed."

Jacklin looked set to scowl. "I'd say so. You pulled how many of them out of the water?"

"Fifteen."

"And what do you think's going to happen next?" the FEMA man asked. "Somebody's going to want a piece of our hides for the stunt that was pulled. Blowing up that bird was bad enough, but you left a bunch of American citizens stranded in the middle of the ocean."

"You're referring, I take it, to some covert operation to retrieve the scientists."

"A strong possibility," Hill said. "Considering the kind of force we used in three different cities to get most of the heat off us as we flew out."

"A counterattack is something we have discussed," the North Korean said. "We will deal with that if and when it transpires."

Wallace listened as the colonel laid it out. He'd heard the plan before when he'd signed on, but each time it was repeated it sounded even crazier than before. Good thing he was on board for the money, so they could dream up the coming nightmare all they wanted and hopefully leave him be. Once paid, he'd find his own way home from North Korea. He knew a few of the names of the Pentagon brass who had either been ex-

torted or freely joined the council as shadow members
who were on call. They were in the wings and poised
for the time when the Doomsday Army, as he thought
of it, would return to America. Armed with nuke backpacks—created in North Korea—and special cases
containing nerve agents, among other ghastly bio-
weapons—they would roll into selected American
cities. The plan was to hold the White House hostage
while trusted members of the Pentagon seized the reins
of power right under the very roof of the Oval Office.
The more he thought about, the crazier it sounded—no,
it was suicide—but he was stuck to do the colonel's bidding for the present until he could figure out his next
move.

None of the council, however, was supposed to be on
the ride back to North Korea, and the FEMA man was
quick to point that out. A complication, since they were
supposed to be in place when the bombs started going
off again in America. Part of the scheme counted on
American citizens taking to the streets, martial law
being declared and FEMA taking over to restore order.

"So, what are you asking of us, Colonel?" Hill
wanted to know. "Hang in there, we might hit another
bump or two in the road, but the future is still bright?"

The smile was slow in coming, and Wallace wondered if Chongjin was considering whom he could make
an example out of. "Essentially, yes. It will take perhaps
another few months than we originally planned."

"A few months?" Jacklin growled.

"A little more time and we will have at least three
functioning and reliable ICBMs."

Wallace figured it was his turn. "And my role and that of my men, Colonel?"

"Once an exact timetable has been worked out, you and your men will be part of the frontline soldiers who will return to America."

It was all Wallace could do to keep from erupting. Committing suicide wasn't part of the plan.

"I realize this is very sudden, but I hope you have no objections to your new role, Mr. Wallace."

"A pay raise come with this new assignment?"

"But of course."

He'd see about that, he thought. If the colonel didn't come through with the cash, well, there might be a number of ways he could sabotage the operation. For now he'd have to steam in silence. He hadn't come this far to blow it for himself.

The North Korean considered him little more than some sacrificial lamb.

"Sounds like a winner, Colonel," Wallace said.

THE FIRST BLAST CAUGHT Bolan off guard, the soldier flinching at the sudden thunder and brilliant flash. Number-two explosion vaporized the building to fiery matchsticks, coming on the heels of the initial fireball, further shredding their numbers. Clear enough to Bolan he was in the right place. Tolley must have something worth getting killed over.

Bolan figured at least ten hardmen were down as he moved out, his M-16 opening up to starting mopping up staggering blacksuits. He'd glimpsed Tolley's flying leap, the man clearing the brunt of the double whammy by a heartbeat. He didn't know if he was still alive.

The Executioner mowed down three hardmen with a burst of autofire, hitting them left to right. They were shouting, picking themselves up near ground zero, dazed as hell—and turning his way now as he hit level ground. The vehicles became a focal point of cover for blacksuits.

Bolan tapped the M-203's trigger and caught them on the run. He blew the last vehicle on his far left into their faces, broken mannequins sailing back into the storm of debris floating down. The soldier grabbed cover behind the GMC as they came out the smoke and blaze, SMGs erupting, slugs drumming off metal, slashing the earth near Bolan. If Tolley was still in the game, Bolan figured he would gladly accept a little help.

TOLLEY WAS BRIEFLY amazed he was still breathing. Rubble pelted him, but he couldn't make out any sound through the ringing in his ears. Something was happening, though, as he looked up over his rock wall. Three, then four shadows dropped before one of their trucks was blasted into scrap.

A big silhouette was on the move, tall, moving like an athlete, or as if he knew this kind of drill so well it was second nature.

Belasko.

The one-man cavalry had arrived, and Tolley wasn't about to see the guy snuffed now, not after laying it on the line for him.

With his HK-33 up and tracking, Tolley hit two of the

blacksuit goons with a rising burst up their spines as they tried to fall in for cover between the vehicles. It was hard to tell with all the smoke how many were left, but there were enough men to pin Belasko down.

The only way he could see ending it, coming out the other side in one piece, was to wade in and catch the survivors in a scissors with Belasko. A few rounds to announce himself, and he was banking Belasko would pick it up a notch.

Tolley rolled over the top edge of the rock wall and went for broke, sweeping the assault rifle up the line of blacksuits.

THEY WERE TORN between two shooters, as Tolley showed himself in a blaze of autofire, blacksuits undecided which way to turn and blast their SMGs. It was enough hesitation on their part, long enough for Bolan to arm a frag grenade and lob it around the corner of his GMC cover.

Three blacksuits scrambled to clear the blast, eyes filling with fear, when two of them were knocked off their feet as the steel egg blew.

With Tolley striking them from behind, Bolan rolled out, his M-16 flaming and cutting two more down. Two moaning men reared up from the strewed wreckage, bloody shadows reeling just beyond the band of fire where the propane tank had been ignited. They triggered short bursts from their subguns before Bolan kicked them off their feet.

He was searching the killzone for any more surprises, moving to meet Tolley halfway down the line of GMCs.

"I think we got them all. Belasko, I hope?"

Bolan nodded, then looked at the man who he hoped had some solid answers about the council.

"That wasn't too shabby for a Justice agent," Tolley said. "Looked like you knew what you were doing."

"I've had a little experience with this sort of thing."

"Well, we might want to ride out of here," Tolley said, "in case there's backup in the area. Your wheels or mine?"

"Mine," the Executioner said.

The soldier was leading the way back to his Crown Victoria, retrieving his war bag, when a shroud of light stabbed the gloom up beyond the incline.

Tolley cursed. "Looks to me like the night just got longer."

"WHAT'S GOING to become of us, Thomas? What's going to happen?"

They were sitting on the lower bunk, Shaw not answering his wife right away, instead turning his head and checking on his daughter. She was curled up in a fetal position, sleeping. Exhausted by terror, no doubt, and Shaw couldn't help but feel any number of mixed feelings. Sure, they were alive, and he was damn grateful for that, but the horror was watching in helpless rage as the North Korean colonel left the others to the angry whims of the ocean or shooting them like rats in a barrel for shark bait.

"I wish to God I knew," he told her.

"Our own people won't just leave us prisoners in a foreign country?"

"Not after what's happened. Listen, we have to hang in there, help each other stay strong, Becky."

He looked around at the cramped bunk, barely enough room to stand and stretch. Nothing he could see but dark bulkheads, but he couldn't help but wonder if the North Korean was watching or listening.

If he was eavesdropping, it wouldn't surprise Shaw.

He was as frightened as his wife and daughter, of course, but he was surprised he was holding up. Hope, he supposed, was all they had. And he had to wonder if their own government would find a way to rescue them. The longer the nightmare lasted would push them all toward some nervous breakdown. Now they were dressed like common criminals in coveralls, forced earlier to undress in front of each other. Humiliation and horror kept piling up, and he knew his wife was scared to death of whatever was next. What could he say? What could he do? He had no answers, but she must've read his thoughts behind his long stare. If only she knew how sorry he was. He wanted to blame himself for not being more careful somehow, perhaps reading the signs that treachery was afoot, tipped off by the traitor, Christopher Blankenship, a fellow SDI scientist. He wanted to tell her he would somehow make up for years of neglecting her, that his one wish was for all of them to be free, home and safe again with their other daughter, Sara, who had escaped when the men came. He only wanted another chance.

She reached out and touched his face. "Someone will come for us, I know they will."

"I know. We're more useful to them alive but only

as long as we help them advance their nuclear missile program."

"Are you going to help them?"

"I don't have much choice. Doing what they want..."

"Or they'd kill us."

"Yes. Come here."

He took her in his arms, embracing her tight. Despite the terror over the future, it was good to hold her, give her whatever comfort he could. It occurred to him anything could go wrong. Subs were notoriously unpredictable, subject to any manner of accident or malfunction, and he was unaware that the North Koreans even had a nuclear-powered submarine. For all he knew, it could simply be a bucket of bolts ready to come apart. There was a chance they might not even make it to North Korea.

He felt her shudder in his arms, thinking this could be the last time he ever held his wife.

4

Getting safely to the rental car and the hell out of there was out of the question. Four hardmen had it covered, waiting for his return, their GMC having slid in right beside his wheels, shadows out and armed with SMGs, bodies aimed his direction. And Bolan found two more trucks were on the prowl. Figure twelve more shooters, then, and any edge they'd achieved by blowing up those shooters who went to the door, or nailing them in a cross fire was out the window. Retreat wasn't an option in his mind, although they could make Tolley's wheels and try to launch a hard run across the desert.

Logic told him this bunch was the last of them, the reserve squad waiting to see how it went right off the bat. It suited Bolan more to stand and fight than risk a blown tire over the broken desert terrain where they could be stranded out in the open and picked off. Whoever had called the shots there had made some serious miscalculations in deployment of troops. If they'd known about him all along, Bolan figured he should have seen them long before he made his move to bail out Tolley. They should have hit him from behind instead of waiting it out, then showing up. Figure arrogance or belief the odds were well on their side, but Bolan had bigger worries right then other than who or why the enemy team had mucked its play.

"Let's move," Bolan said as he crouched and headed up the side of the hill. They were made, but no shots were fired their way, no foot troops moving in. So far. The GMCs were going in opposite directions, keeping a decent distance from the hills, and Bolan then figured they'd left a scout somewhere behind. Which probably meant they knew the score and the numbers. The Executioner armed the M-203 with a frag bomb, then hunkered down in a shallow depression.

"Call me crazy, but I think they know we're here," Tolley said, falling in beside Bolan. "What's the plan?"

"You must have something pretty damn important for them to send a full platoon of hitters."

"Maybe the end of a free American society."

"We can talk about it later—if we make it out of here."

The moment begged the question, where did they come from? Bolan knew there was a number of restricted military bases spread around California. And even Edwards Air Base could be compromised, he knew, if that's where this killing bunch had come from. No time to ponder that dilemma now.

Bolan saw the trucks slowing, then stop. Two armed shadows fell out of each vehicle, and the way in which they moved on the hill told him they were going for a pincers attack. Choke them off from both sides, end of game.

"Only one way to do this," the soldier told Tolley.

"Meet them head-on?"

"You got it."

"You didn't strike me as the running type."

"Not my style."

"So which ones do we hit first?"

Bolan was considering splitting up, but if Tolley went down, this run was all for nothing. No, Bolan would keep his intel gold mine right beside him, no matter what. He was just about to move out to tackle the team to the north when a voice he'd been hoping to hear from patched through.

"Partyhawk to Striker, come in."

Bolan grabbed his radio. Voices carried in the desert so he kept his tone down to a harsh whisper. "Tell me you're in the neighborhood."

"On the way. I'm thinking you've got problems."

"About twelve of them."

"I'm three miles and counting off."

"Take out everything on the ground, vehicles, hostiles, the works, but leave the north end of the hills to me. Sweep the south end for two more hostiles while you're at it."

"Roger."

"The cavalry's on the way?" Tolley asked.

"We might just get lucky yet. Come on," Bolan said before heading for higher ground.

MARK CARRUTHERS KNEW the stakes. If the bastard from the DIA was allowed to hand over the information he had on the Phoenix Council, along with all the critical recruiting data, the who, why and when on the mercenary army, then the former Delta Force commando knew they were all so screwed they might as well lie down and die under the blistering sun of the Mojave Desert. Ominous rumblings were already blowing their way from Nellis, which meant if and when certain power players went under the microscope, it might not be long before the rest of them started feeling the heat.

He had a job to do. It had taken months of shadowing Tolley, tracking him by following the credit-card trail, but the old desert rat, Kearnes, had been known to them. Common sense and some checking on their respective pasts told the boss man in charge of Fort Irwin's Area 63 they were co-workers, buddies at the DIA, so he steered them right to the old-timer's doorstep. They had been watching the place for days, monitoring all calls around the clock, and Carruthers had been itching for some action, tired of sweating it out under the sun, waiting for their mark to come out and do something.

Well, Tolley had done something, all right, and it could mean the end of the Phoenix Council unless this mess was cleaned up pronto.

And it looked as if he would get some action, after all.

At first, during the night's briefing, Carruthers had been galled to think this many seasoned warriors were needed to come out there and round up one backstabber. Then the intercepted calls to the Justice Department were made known to him. Help from D.C. was on the way. That help had arrived, apparently, and the reports from their scout to the south made it sound as if one guy had shown up to aid and assist in waxing twenty-something of his comrades as if they were cherries fresh out of OCS. He found it all unbelievable to the point of absurd, but they were losing men hard and fast to only two shooters.

With Ballard beside him, they began trekking up the north face of the hills, quietly as they could without kicking stones around, their MP-5s fanning the night. Enough glow from the reported firestorm illuminated the ridgeline, marking the way without the need for night-vision goggles. Their scouts had marked the position of the quarry, south and holding. Two guys, no problem, he thought, then he spied the destruction on the far side of the hill. Tolley had mined his shack, putting pressure plates on the stoop and blowing more than half their guys away in the opening eyeblink. He took in the sprawled bodies around the smoking debris. If it had been Carruthers's call, he would not have hung back the reserve force near the interstate. They'd seen the Crown Victoria with Tolley's rescuer going down the road, but the orders were to let him ride on. Looking back, it made no sense. They should have shot the bastard as soon as he showed or at least ridden in hard on his ass, blasting away as soon as he stepped out, a mere G-man ready to throw around his weight. He was on the hunt for their quarry with a tac radio, but strict radio silence had been ordered. That meant there was no way of knowing if the other guys were on the move right then. It was as if the major thought sheer numbers and audacity alone could win this one. So far, they were losing, and losing badly.

Orders were orders, he knew, and he intended to carry them through. There were powerful men who handed off large cash sums for his role as security force in the council to do what he was told, when he was told. Beyond the council's wishes, he had his own future to consider. Such as early retirement, a place in the mountains, maybe write his memoirs.

That was tomorrow; right then he needed to concentrate.

The big shadow boiled up out of nowhere, rising from the ridgeline like some dark phantom from hell. Carruthers was bringing his subgun to bear on the ghost and attempting a darting shuffle to the side, but he already knew it was too late. He wondered why in the hell nobody had seen the guy on the move to intercept him, damn the radio silence, when the muzzle of the shadow's assault gun began to flame, opening up his guts with hot lead.

THE AH-1F COBRA HAD everything Jack Grimaldi could ask for to drop the hammer from above and clean up Bolan's troubles on the ground. The fire-control system was a state-of-the-art digital ballistic computer, a thing of beauty. The HUD—Heads-Up Display— brought it all into focus down there, allowing him to target and control the weapons systems by helmet sight unit. And this machine, he knew, was armed with enough firepower to turn those hills into a lake of fire. Chin-mounted GE universal turret with 30 mm Gatling guns, for starters, then there were eight laser-guided TOW antitank missiles on the wing pylons. A tank killer, for sure, plenty enough wallop to decimate a small army. Plus the enemy knew he wasn't locking in from their blind side. Before they spotted him it would be way too late.

Despite feeling shaky and rough around the edges from a week of sun and fun in Miami Beach, Jack Grimaldi was up to the task. Hell, he'd been looking to get back to work for days, tired of idling around on the beach. The country had been blowing up all around him, terrorists landing on American shores, and once Grimaldi caught wind of Bolan's role he was game for action.

And the timing couldn't have been any better. His old friend needed a helping hand.

No sweat.

He cut back on the speed, range about a hundred meters now, shadows around the truck looking his way. Grimaldi let it rip.

"WHAT DO YOU INTEND to do about them? They ask too many questions. They worry too much. Men who are on the verge of panic are, in my experience, like dangerous animals."

Colonel Chongjin drummed his fingers on the table. He was alone now with Commander Ohm in the wardroom. The Americans had been dismissed to their bunks, grumbling on the way out about the whole sudden change in the operation. Fretting and anxious. Concerned only about themselves. Well, just what was he supposed to tell them anyway? There was no crystal ball, no way to guarantee any man's future. The whole deviation from the original scheme had been forced upon them by a covert force that had struck at their heels in Oklahoma, driving them like herded cattle to endure the entire journey now and what would be their eventual holding-over phase in his country. It happened. Deal with it.

Or else.

It was up to them, of course, if they wanted to stay with the program, and Chongjin sincerely hoped they stuck it out. But any more squawking about their own personal futures and he wouldn't hesitate to order them executed. Once they landed safely at port in Haeju, he would secure the SDI scientists on the base, put them to work, house and feed them and their families. There were also the Iraqis to deal with, the envoy who was right then waiting on North Korean soil for his return. There was the matter of ongoing technology exchange, with weapons grade U-235 and P-239 among other reactor component parts, chemical and biological weapons to safely smuggle into Iraq. It was part of the agreement they had with Iraq's president for extending them his jihad army.

There were problems to solve, yes. Not to mention Kim Jong Il, who would prove a thorn in his side at some future point. The buffoon was still leader of the DPRK, having given his blessing to the venture, but soon enough, if all went according to the plan to storm the palace, Chongjin and his army of officers would dictate the future of not only their own country but eventually the world.

He was getting ahead of himself. Commander Ohm wanted specifics, but Chongjin could only think to say, "We wait and see what they do. Perhaps they will come to their senses and realize there is no choice but to endure."

"The Americans will send a black-ops team to get them back."

"Let them come. We'll be ready to deal with anything they send. Too much time, risk and expense has already gone into this whole operation to simply turn our backs on our American counterparts. Should the American members of the council be successful in unleashing their cutthroat army on their cities, while taking over the political, intelligence and military infrastructure, they will own their country. Our own handlers will be by their side then, dictating our terms."

Commander Ohm didn't look convinced to Chongjin. "So, what does it all come down to, Colonel, in the event our country is attacked?"

"It's very simple. It's us or them. And if I can't bargain with the lives of the scientists, I will have them all killed."

"Then it was all for nothing."

"It is never for nothing. If we are forced to, we will stand our ground and die fighting if necessary. And in the worst-case scenario, I have the codes to launch the warheads we have in Haeju. If all else fails, I will find a way to make one final statement to our enemies."

Chongjin ignored the dark look falling over Ohm's face. If the commander had problems following orders, Chongjin also had a solution where he was concerned.

THEY LOOKED SHOCKED to see him, eyes going wide, mirroring the firelight behind him. Bolan didn't waste a second letting them feel too much—except the sweeping burst of autofire he chewed them up with. Tolley joined the bloody savaging of the blacksuited duo. They were tumbling back down the hill when Bolan heard, then saw, the Cobra vectoring in from the west and cutting loose with a missile-Gatling gun combo.

The night blew up once again.

The gunners around his rental car didn't stand a chance. The pounding blew them apart, limbs vanishing in dark bursts. The TOW slammed into the GMC and sealed their doom, wreckage taking to the sky with flying body parts.

Bolan led Tolley down the hillside, alert for any movement that might come out of the night in any direction. The Executioner watched as Grimaldi kept on working. The Cobra sailed for the south end and hovered as Grimaldi lined them up in infrared tracking. The thunderous retort of 30 mm Gatling guns sounded. The hillside erupted in huge belching clouds of smoke and dust and whatever else—bodies—that got in the way of its strafing doom.

As he closed on the flaming scrap of the GMC, the Executioner discovered one of the blacksuits clinging to a final few breaths.

Grimaldi patched through, indicating they were clear, then informed Bolan there was a truck to the south.

"Take it out. Then pick us up."

The order copied, the Executioner closed on the hardmen. Bolan rolled on, combat senses torqued up, spying the hills and the desert for any hidden shadows. The hardman was in the process of reaching for his HK subgun when Bolan kicked it away.

"Which base are you from?"

The man looked up, cursing. "Irwin."

"You the last of them?"

"For now. You think you can stop what's happening, you don't know shit."

"I know enough."

"Right. What else do you want to know?"

"That's it," the Executioner said, and drilled a 3-round mercy burst into his head.

Bolan stepped away from the hungry flames and scoured the wasteland. He heard the distant peals of thunder, then Grimaldi patched through. "All done, Sarge. Nothing but you two is showing up my screen."

The soldier and Tolley waited a full minute or so, then Grimaldi flew in and settled the Cobra on its landing skids. Bolan hopped through the hatch and found Grimaldi twisted around in his seat, grinning.

"I know, I know. Good to see me, Sarge."

"Get us out of here, but let's do a sweep of the area. Find someplace you can set us down so I can talk to Tolley."

Grimaldi gave Bolan a thumbs-up, then lifted off.

"We're going to have a talk," Bolan told Tolley, then settled down to the sat link modem Grimaldi had brought with him from the Farm.

5

"Papua New Guinea? Are you jerking my chain, Tolley?"

"I'm afraid not."

Brognola's voice shot out the speakerphone over the sat link. The big Fed's tone of angry disbelief, though, echoed Bolan's own sentiments about what Tolley had spilled so far regarding the so-called Doomsday Army. Beyond the lash in Brognola's voice, his old friend sounded edgy, nerves shot all to hell. Understandable, given not only what had happened to American citizens so far, but also Tolley's story about the planned nightmare on the horizon. There was a heavy pause, both ends of the conversation gathering their thoughts, sifting through it, the mad ambition of evil men. The silence beyond the grounded Cobra—where Grimaldi had set it down on a salt flat near the Cady Mountains following a thirty-minute sweep of the vicinity—seemed to weigh down on the warbird with some oppressive force. It left Bolan filled with hot anger over the who's who list of traitors on their side and a seething impatience to get on with the business of taking down this Doomsday Army. Grimaldi was just inside the cockpit hatch, monitoring the screens for signs of life in the area.

"After what's happened I wouldn't think anything would surprise you people," Tolley finally said, working on a cigarette, the man's hand shaking as if he needed something stronger to calm the postbattle jitters. "These guys have been playing God for a long time. They practically run the country, damn near the whole intelligence and military infrastructure. And they're ready to topple the whole goddamn country, even if that means taking the entire White House hostage and laying waste to entire cities. With FEMA declaring martial law, you've got the director and assistant director, the whole higher chain of command there ready to use this Doomsday Army to seal it for them."

"Okay, let's slow down," Brognola said. "Let's start from the beginning. How did they manage to snap up this huge chunk of jungle real estate—in where?"

"The Western Province," Tolley said. "It's the least populated area of PNG, borders the Indonesian West Irian. You've got swamp, jungle, the Fly River..."

"With mosquitoes the size of crows and saltwater crocs, okay I catch the Discovery channel once in a blue moon. They're sealed off, embraced by the landscape. Now, how in the world could they slash and burn out the jungle to plop down a sprawling complex, complete with airfields, hangars, machine-gun batteries and a hundred or so mercenaries, training on mock-ups for urban warfare and shooting up targets without anybody raising a stink?"

"By anybody, I assume," Tolley said, "you mean the national parliament in Port Moresby."

"Whatever. You mean to tell me our own people bought off the British monarch over there? What about the Aussies? Correct me if I'm wrong, but Australia should get a little nervous about a large mercenary army in Papua New Guinea, since last I believe I heard they dump more financial aid into the PNG than anybody else."

"It happened. Top to bottom, there was huge funneling of dirty money, greasing the skids all around, see no evil, like that. A lot of the funds came from Pyongyang when the Phoenix Council was being chosen or forced to join, part of Colonel Chongjin's war chest from the chem and bio weapons, some techno goodies he gave the Iraqi president, what he could hide that was, from Kim Jong and his cronies. And those nuke backpacks I understand they have? Courtesy of North Korea. Our guys, the snakes, as you call them, shelled out huge bucks to get their hands on them. I've heard they're just like the suitcase kind the Green Berets use, only they pack a bigger kiloton punch."

Brognola cursed. "Where the hell have our intelligence people been the past couple of years? We don't know the first damn thing about North Korean nuke backpacks."

"The right—or wrong ones—have been in bed with the North Koreans. Hey, I'm just the messenger here. You're getting the names and the facts now," Tolley said. "Check it."

"You're right, I'll check it, and I can't believe some of these names I'm seeing."

"By the way, I understand how the game is played, but I've been talking to you for two days now and I don't have a name."

"Call me Albert," Brognola growled. "Whoever gave you this number knew my name, that's all you need to know."

Bolan understood his friend had been under fire since this campaign started, but he felt it was time to intervene and lay out a plan of attack. "Whatever we have here, I've seen enough to know they can—or at least think they can—pull it off."

"And don't forget," Tolley said, "the classified spooks up at Irwin marched out the heavy hitters to eighty-six me. You want proof, that should do it. Hey, gentlemen, I don't want to feel like I, and you, Belasko, stuck our necks out to see these traitors gas and nuke American cities. If that happens, this whole country will explode and there will be anarchy in the streets. Martial law, Apocalypse, U.S.A. What happened in Chicago and L.A. is small time compared to what these bastards have lined up next."

"Nobody's doubting what you're laying on us," Brognola said.

"Okay, I understand, it's a lot to swallow at once. Shakes the hell out of your belief in the so-called good guys," Tolley said. "Hell, that our system can become so compromised by a few assholes holding the reins."

"Oh, that doesn't even begin to touch it, friend," Brognola said, looking at the file that was e-mailed to him. "Okay, I'm reading as fast as I can. You're telling me all these classified military flights were actually flown out of the SDI compound in Oklahoma? I'm looking at Bolling and Irwin just to name a few."

"Men and matériel," Tolley said. "I was brought on board to help with gathering supplies, weapons and to make some flight arrangements, sort of a double cutout for one of the Pentagon hotshots. I found out the uglier stuff, like the chem and bio packages, were being handled by a colleague of mine at the DIA. They came out of experimental laboratories much like the one of Area 51 fame. Now, the recruiting took some finagling and a little time. It was forged Department of Defense letterhead that went out to potential recruits. Computers can do anything these days, you know. They had P.O. boxes and sent months of correspondence. Nothing on the Internet that could nail them by the Feds. It's about half-and-half, fifty percent former legit soldiers from various branches. Bottom of the barrel really, as far as society is concerned. Burnouts, some Section Eights, some with criminal records, but they have combat experience and killing in their blood. Men with no futures, no hope, on the run from the law, desperate for money. The rest, I understand, were wanna-bes, cannon fodder. You have names, check them. You'll find they've all up and disappeared, a few of the wanna-bes leaving behind a dead spouse or girlfriend. Some sort of initiation rite, I guess, when the recruiters come knocking on the door. Or it was a way to get them locked into the deal. No way out."

"I have to ask, Tolley," Brognola said, "why come to us this late in the game?"

"What can I tell you! I was writing a book!" Tolley snapped. He fell silent, looked at Bolan, then said,

"Sorry. It's been a tough night, I'm a little stressed. Hey, you guys wouldn't happen to have a shot of booze on this bird?"

"In the bag right below the sat link," Grimaldi told Bolan, who bent, zipped it open and handed Tolley a bottle of Seagram's.

The man worked on the bottle like a desert wanderer who hadn't tasted water in days. A few moments later his hands stopped shaking. "Thanks, I needed that. Anyway, that was always my plan, Albert," Tolley said, lighting up another cigarette off his dying butt, tossing the gnawed butt on the floorboard, grinding it out beneath his foot. "They thought they had me in the beginning. I had an affair, they threatened to go to my wife and ruin my career, but they didn't know my marriage was already on the ropes. I played ball, did the dirty work, was part of the gang. But I was always looking to nail these bastards at some point. I wasn't sure how. I guess sticking it to them was my way of holding on to my last shred of pride. Those names you're seeing? It took time to get all this stuff together for you, one reason it may look I dragged my feet. Anyway, the ones at the top, well, it was a mixed bag of reasons, I gather. Some joined freely, the usual rhetoric, America's going to hell, need to do something drastic, some out of sheer arrogance to show the world they're a little smarter than everybody else. Money, naturally, brought more than a few on deck. Then there was some fair amount of extortion, the colonel using Korean women, the sex thing...."

"Well, that much fits," Brognola said. "To add to

that, Striker, those videos are turning up a lot of rats with dirty habits all over Washington. I've got senators, Pentagon brass, NSA, DIA...it boggles my mind to think so many we trust would fall so deep into the toilet."

"Suggestion on that front," Bolan said. "Hold off taking any action on your end."

"You mean wait while these traitors go on about the business of maybe knocking off the President or his whole cabinet?"

"Sound the alert to the Man. Keep it quiet, keep an eye on anybody on the list who might get close to him. Have your people shadow the bigger snakes—it might lead to their North Korean handlers or whoever else is lurking in the dark."

"You want these bastards yourself?"

"See how it plays, but what you have now should clear the way for us to tackle two fronts and mop them up. I'm thinking the ones on this end will keep for a while until Chongjin gets further along advancing the North Korean nuke missile program or whenever this Doomsday Army makes its way back into the States. In that case, I'm thinking months before they're even ready to strike here again. Here's what I want."

And Bolan put the surgical strikes to Brognola. He wanted two squads of blacksuits, massive air firepower to pave the way for the ground troops and to get a U.S. aircraft carrier involved if possible. They could hammer out the details when they knew more about numbers and compound layouts. Constant satellite watching of two AIQs, Papua New Guinea and the suspected dock site for the sub. Get the whole package put together ten min-

utes ago, and Bolan and company go in and raze this
jungle outpost first. Figure with a day to two days to
hammer it down in Papua New Guinea, and by then the
colonel's sub would have surfaced in port. Use the
enemy's own base of operations on Papua New Guinea
as a launching point to go into North Korea. Forget political fallout, the DMZ, it was time to strike back.

"It shouldn't be a hard sell at this stage," Bolan said.
"North Korea has essentially declared war on the United
States. Maybe Kim Jong Il will get nervous and take
care of Chongjin himself."

"And hand back our own people, all's well?" Brognola said.

"I doubt it. Extreme measures, nothing short," Bolan
said. "We have to move fast, take some big chances.
Make it happen, the Man knows the men I'll take are
the most deniable expendables around. We'll get it done.
We'll work out the details as we get there. Partyhawk?"
he called out to Grimaldi. "What do you think you might
need to open the door for us to crash the house on
PNG?"

Grimaldi looked from Bolan to Tolley. "Depends. If
they have antiaircraft batteries, SAMS..."

"None," Tolley said. "They don't even use radar."

Bolan and Grimaldi stared at Tolley.

"You're kidding?" Grimaldi said.

"The CMFs use their own frequency tied into the
PNG commander. They clear them on the way in."

"Cocky bastards," Grimaldi said.

"They think they're untouchable," Tolley said. "Hey,
I know what they have. I helped arrange the ordnance."

"Okay," Grimaldi said, "something big, mean and nasty. A Spectre should do real nice. I'll need a crew of our own people to help me out."

"I'm looking at a full day or more to get you guys at the back door and with what you need. I've got to clear all this with the President," Brognola said. "You know, I have to say this, Tolley. All this time, all these snakes slithering over each other, and no one broke down, not one guilty conscience. Conspiracies usually come unraveled because somebody talks."

"And that would be me, the talker. I can't speak for the others. Pride, the money, fear, who knows what kept them going. It happened and it's still happening."

"You guys get to Edwards," Brognola said. "I'll have a ride waiting for you. I'm thinking a base in Hawaii, close enough until I can get our people to work out the particulars."

"I want in when you hit PNG," Tolley announced.

Bolan shot Tolley a look, wondering if the booze was talking for him.

"I don't think that's a good idea," Brognola said, "I need you close—we need to check all this out."

"I've seen the satellite imagery of the area. I know the layout, where they keep the doomsday packages. You go in there blasting and bombing away, well, it'll be hard enough getting to their back door in sweltering hundred-plus heat without lumbering through the jungle in HAZMAT suits."

"Striker?"

"I'll take him with me for now. We'll talk more about it when we're ready to go."

"Then I need to get busy here."

As Brognola signed off and Grimaldi fired up the warbird, Bolan watched Tolley sucking on the bottle.

"I'm being straight, Belasko. It's all true, every dirty, ugly scrap of it."

Bolan nodded. "That's the trouble I'm having. I believe you."

SENATOR DARREN STERLING, Democrat from Oklahoma, felt himself coming apart to the point of hysterical panic, his body racked, head to toe, with tremors brought on by the nightmare his life had become.

"Oh, God, you can't do this. You can't just make me disappear. It's morning, I'm due at the Hill, there are meetings...."

"You'll do what we want."

He collapsed on the edge of the bed, choked down on the sob, his face dropping in his hands. They had him, bought and sold like the Korean whore he'd killed—his whole world spinning off its axis, flying away before his very eyes and all over a piece of ass.

This wasn't happening, he told himself. But it was. He still couldn't believe he'd killed Su Lin. Worse, they had the whole sordid scene on tape. There was more video, of course, the kind of activity that would nail him to a public crucifixion, and that's what had jump-started the nightmare. Since he'd accidentally killed Su Lin— hitting her after she slapped him, the whore cracking open her skull on the edge of the bar in her hotel suite— he hadn't been able to eat, sleep or concentrate on his work. His two handlers, one North Korean, the other an

American with a blondish buzz cut, had only left his side when he'd gone to his office at the Hill, warning him his phone was tapped and his office bugged.

He was in his McLean, Virginia, home now, wishing he didn't have to go anywhere that morning. He was disheveled, unshaven, with bags under his eyes. He needed to sleep, desperately, wake up in a few days and find this was all just a bad dream. Wherever he went now he imagined everyone—from aides, colleagues to folks on the street or in restaurants—was staring at him, wondering about him, reading his paranoia and guilt, plain as day. Oh, God, he was falling apart.

"Pull yourself together, Senator," the spook he knew as Mr. John told him. "You'll have your kind of company where we're going."

"Why do this? You don't think anybody's going to wonder?"

"It has to be done. We discovered a serious enough leak in the chain of our own operatives to believe a number of our—you'll forgive the expression—pigeons could be snatched up by the Justice Department."

He looked up, his jaw falling, a fresh jolt of terror ripping through him. "What? I'm going to be arrested?"

"Not if you do exactly what you are told. Two, three days tops, and you should be able to return to your office."

"My God, man, do you know what's happened? The country has been under a terrorist siege, American citizens kidnapped by North Koreans...."

"That's why we need to get you and few others to a safehouse. We need to determine which way the winds are going to blow."

"Oh, God. My wife, she'll wonder what's happening."

"Forget about her. You've never had a problem before now neglecting or outright ignoring the little lady."

"You..."

"Bastard? No, Senator, consider me your savior, your only ticket to keep what you have. Career. All the good life. Let's go. If I have to stand here much longer and listen to you whine, I'm going to puke."

"I need to pack."

"No." Mr. John grabbed him by the arm and yanked him to his feet. "Just as you are. Move it."

He felt his knees shaking, bile shooting up his throat. He was finished, life as he knew it down the drain. There would be public disgrace. Worse, he feared he was facing a long stretch in prison. There was bribery and all manner of fraud and collusion. Oh, God, they would even brand him a traitor for going along with whatever their scheme was. Life without parole, no pardon for him, not with this administration.

He was on the verge of hyperventilating when he saw the North Korean standing in the living room and heard someone at the wet bar rattling ice cubes in a glass. He was moving deeper into the living room, wondering who else was under the roof when...

"Have a drink first, Senator. Get your nerves together."

He stood, paralyzed. He couldn't believe it, but there he was, holding out a drink, wearing the full uniform of a Marine brigadier general. The very same brigadier general from the Pentagon's Fifth Ring he'd worked with on the Senate Committee on Counterterrorism.

"Like the man said," the brigadier general told him.

"You'll be in good company soon, your kind of people. Take this and drink up."

He nearly toppled, fainting, but he felt Mr. John grab him by the shoulders and steer him toward the bar.

6

Rupert Hadley had no idea where he really was, but he wished to God he were back in Colorado. As ridiculous as it sounded in his mind, he even missed the constant verbal assaults by his girlfriend, longing for the whole dead-end life of being a shiftless, part-time drug-dealing wild man in the mountains. The trouble was, there was no going back. Not unless he wished to face a murder rap, life in the big house for damn sure for shooting her before he'd gone with the two men allegedly from the Department of Defense.

His former life back in the States might have been ugly and sordid, but the present was pure hell. Even still, he supposed it was better than prison, but not by much.

It was the end of his second full day, somewhere in a jungle, and he was hating life. If this was some sort of military training, he didn't want any part of it. They were running in place again—all they did was run—the drill instructor—or whatever he was supposed to be—barking at the other ten guys he'd seen on the plane ride, moving down the line, hurling curses, shouting in their faces. The Barker, that's how he thought of the guy, but he wasn't about to call him that, at least not to his face. The lean guy in the green khakis and undershirt was lugging a big silver .45-caliber pistol on his hip, and he looked as if he wouldn't hesitate to use it.

"Let's go, ladies, hit it! Drop and eat some dirt, you no-good, wanna-be sacks of shit!"

Again, belly flopping to the soft earth that smelled like rotting garbage.

"Up!"

Clambering to his feet, head spinning from exertion, queasy bile churning in his belly.

"Drop!"

Hitting the ground, thinking much more of this and he'd lose his guts and his quaking bowels. Run, run, run. Sit-ups, push-ups, bombarded the whole time by the Barker's insults, the guy proving he was pretty creative in that regard, Hadley had to give him that. Like the others, he was wheezing, baking under the sun. It was hotter than ever, even though the sun was starting to sink beyond the black volcanic tableland. He was a piece of human suet, out of shape from years of self-indulgence, no question, his body a toxic waste dump, every pore like a faucet wide open to wash him head to toe in oily sweat. Well, the chow wasn't too shabby, some kind of beef stew, cakes and oranges for dessert. The three smoke breaks during the day were something to look forward to, but other than that, if he had to keep this pace up, he was sure he'd have a heart attack.

And he wanted to go home, on the verge of telling the Barker he wanted out.

"That's enough. Take five," the DI roared. "Stay in formation, goddammit!"

Hadley heaved himself to his feet and heard one of the others puking.

"You girls make me sick. Bunch of goddamn candy-ass civilians. Barroom brawlers, tough guys, huh? Do the *Soldier of Fortune* convention, pop off your hunting rifles and you think you're a bunch of Rambos? I'm here to tell you none of you have shown me a thing that makes me even begin to think you can cut it."

Here we go, Hadley thought, and on went the insults to their manhood, their wives, their mothers, everything under the sun they thought about themselves or might hold near and dear. He let his mind drift, then was jolted by the small-arms and assault-rifle fire out on the range. He was able to focus on something now other than his own misery. Maybe close to a hundred guys in khakis and T-shirts out there, shooting up targets or charging into what looked like small building mock-ups. It all looked somehow official enough, but what was really going on there? What were they training for? How come they couldn't be out there, shooting assault rifles with the others instead of this PT nonsense? He checked it out, trying but failing to drown out the tirade.

The airfield had been slashed out of the jungle. The two choppers, two twin-engine planes, as well as the sleek jet that had brought him there, were all grounded near hangars. Maybe if he'd stayed awake on the ride he could've figured out where he was. Hell, it could have been Borneo or Vietnam for all he knew. Figure some kind of emotional exhaustion after murdering his girl, only he'd been too busy shaking and sweating off all the booze during the flight, falling asleep for hours on end, and that was when he could keep time straight.

Their tent was huge, fifty guys like himself jammed into rows of bunks. Mosquitoes were another constant source of murderous aggravation, big, ravenous bastards that somehow managed to find a way through the netting and eat him up while he lay in his bunk. The past night he couldn't sleep, between the mosquitoes and the jungle making all these eerie howling and cawing noises and other frightening sounds that filtered into whatever bad dreams he managed to find when he could doze off. The Barker and the others with pistols had their own hut, way down at the end of the trail, isolating themselves. Big shots. Then the others, fifty or so in all, had some look of military bearing and experience, and they, too, had their own tin or steel barracks or whatever it was made of. Huge drums of fuel, generators and Humvees spread all over. Machine-gun nests, too, and that made him wonder about what sort of wild-assed natives were in the vicinity. Hell, they could be headhunters for all he knew. He came all this way, risked his life, to end up in some savage's boiling pot?

This sucked.

"So, you girls want to be soldiers, huh? It's going to take me a month just to flush the poison out of your sorry hides."

Someone groaned, "Shit. A month?"

Hadley saw the Barker roll right up into the face of the groaner. "What was that? You say something?" He malingered, nose to nose with the groaner, who looked as if he wished he could disappear into thin air.

"I didn't think so, Judy. That's you from now on. Judy. Crying like some bitch."

"How about our money? I never got paid like I was promised. I was told five grand when I signed on."

Something cold dropped over the Barker's face as he moved down the line. Hadley froze—the malcontent happened to be standing next to him.

"This isn't about money, scumsucker. You'll get paid when you get paid. Are we clear, Wall Street?"

The malcontent, and Hadley gave him some credit since he was wondering about cash himself, pressed the issue.

"I'm afraid not, sir."

"You're what?"

"I said that isn't good enough."

The Barker seemed to think about something, head nodding. "Okay, you're telling me you're not happy here? You're telling me you maybe want to leave?"

"I...well...yes, sir. I've had enough."

"Okay. Anybody else? Any more quitters?"

A freeze went down the line. No takers.

"Okay, honey, hit the airfield. You're free to go."

Hadley glimpsed the man hesitating, then he squeezed past the Barker, who watched him go as if he were the sorriest piece of human dung on the planet. The Barker told the group, "You ladies hit the river and grab a bath. Fifteen minutes then meet me right here. Move out!"

Fifteen minutes, it wasn't much, but Hadley was glad for the briefest break to get out of the Barker's glaring and yelling and insults. He watched the malcontent trudging toward the airfield, his head lowered. Something felt wrong; it was too easy for that man to get dismissed. Hadley looked over his shoulder as he fell in with the others to go down the trail that led to the river. Barker was on his handheld radio. Hadley then listened to the grumbling and grousing the whole march down the trail.

Hadley heard the man next to him say, "You believe this crap? That other guy was right. We were promised money up front, and no one told me I'd end up in the asshole of the world, sweating my tail off. I don't even know where we are. How come the others on the firing range don't have to run all day like us? What, are they special or something?"

Hadley jumped at the distant sound of the pistol shot. He followed the stares of the others toward the airfield. They couldn't see it, but Hadley knew the malcontent just became food for the jungle. This was a nightmare, he thought. They were stuck, and if they wanted out... there was no way out.

He wanted to scream in outrage suddenly, searching the fear clouding the faces of the other recruits. Finally, after some more cursing and griping, they hit the marshy bank of the river. A few of them waded into the brown water. The opposite bank seemed a mile away to Hadley, as he searched the tree line, wondering about hidden savages with blowguns or spears or whatever. They were splashing around, as Hadley ventured a few steps down the bank, nearly slipping in the muddy soup.

"What's your name?"

Hadley looked at the man as he moved into the water, waist high, splashing his face.

"Hadley."

"I'm Johnson. Where you from?"

"Colorado. You?"

"California. I bet they gave you the same song and dance, huh?"

"Yeah, they promised me the world. Taking me away to heaven on earth."

More splashing, Johnson easing a little farther out, up to his chest now.

"Makes you wonder what's really going on here, don't it? I'm thinking this is some kind of mercenary outfit, DOD, my ass."

The man went on grumbling, Hadley checking the water. He didn't like jungle water, never had, since a man couldn't see what might be in it.

Still, despite the greasy, hot feel of the water, he figured it wouldn't hurt to at least wash some of the sweat off his face and neck. He was taking a step into the water, Johnson turning his way when he saw the crocodile.

Hadley knew what it was even as his mind tried to fathom the horror, but he couldn't believe how huge the thing was. It roared up out of the water, big as a small car in his eyes, the scream lashing the air next as its massive jaws clamped down on Johnson.

Hadley slipped and slid back up the bank, a mass exodus of bodies out of the river, yelling and splashing. It wasn't long, maybe two seconds, then Johnson disappeared beneath the surface. A tail thrashed out of the water, Johnson rolling across the surface, screaming, locked in the monster's jaws, then gone for good. A great pool of blood turned the brownish surface into a foamy maelstrom. Hadley scrambled on his haunches up the bank, his own scream locked in his throat.

"Forget about him! He's gone!"

The Barker. Yelling for the others to forget about him, like what? One of them was going back in there to try and play Tarzan?

Hadley somehow found his footing, the thrashing over as the surface settled into a spreading pool of red. He stood and felt the sticky ooze on the seat of his pants where he'd soiled himself. He heard the Barker say, "That was my oversight, people, I take full responsibility for that poor bastard's demise. I forgot to tell you earlier—there are saltwater crocs in this river."

Rupert Hadley hit his knees, buried his face in his hands. He sobbed, ignoring the string of obscenities blasting in his ear.

IT FELT LIKE A DAY and forever since the plan was on the table, but the first of two strikes was finally under way. Bolan was perusing the satellite imagery, as twelve blacksuits from the Farm sat grouped in the belly of the Sea Stallion CH-53, which was on loan from the USS *Enterprise.* Brognola and Stony Man had done little short of performing a logistical miracle to get it to this point.

Wonders from the big Fed and the Farm, Bolan thought, never ceased, but he never doubted their resolve and ability to come through in the crunch of an eleventh hour.

From his layover at Wheeler Air Base in Hawaii, the Farm had quickly found and snapped up an abandoned U.S. Marine base from World War II on the far edge of West New Britain. They got him and the blacksuit team there in record time for this predawn hit. It was close enough to put them at the back door of the enemy's Papua New Guinea compound, a short chopper ferry before the fireworks started.

Bolan had already briefed the troops from the Farm. Shoot to kill, no exceptions. His orders were clear— only take prisoners if they threw their hands up and did little short of begging for their lives on bended knee. The soldier knew he could count on these men to do far more than just follow orders. They were all selected from various branches of service, experienced commandos usually assigned to perform security detail for Stony Man Farm. On occasion they were called into action.

Like now.

This was not a job for Bolan to solo the play. A hundred-plus enemy numbers, but he was counting on Grimaldi and his blacksuit crew in the Spectre to decimate a whopping chunk of the head count.

And the Man had given the green light on both surgical strikes. The USS *Enterprise* had already been tasked to move into the Sea of Japan. Apparently the President had been thinking ahead about a covert foray into North Korea, damn the political backlash. And when he got word about the mercenary army in PNG he had moved fast, executive orders to clear Bolan and allow him carte blanche to call the shots on both fronts.

One strike at a time.

Focus.

They were on the way up the Fly River, ready to land a half klick south of the enemy compound. The Spectre was lagging behind, ready to fly past and lower the boom once Bolan and troops disembarked to leg it in. Besides a few medics, a team of Army HAZMAT specialists was on board the Spectre, ready to deal with the weapons of mass destruction.

That was Bolan's main focus of concern. One mistake, some suicide play by the enemy and their nightmare had only just begun.

Tolley crouched beside the soldier. He was along for the covert war, armed with an M-16/M-203 combo like Bolan and the other troops. His face, neck and hands were blackened with war paint.

"I appreciate you letting me in," Tolley said.

"You're the man knows best about where it all is. I'm counting on your knowledge to keep us from becoming radioactive dust."

Tolley grunted. "Hoping after our stint in the desert I might be a little more than that to you."

"You've helped so far."

"This your way of thanking me?"

"Something like that. You want in, you know the risks."

"Right. Go in, but maybe not out the other side."

"It's your call."

"Stay behind? No, thanks. I'm in. I'm thinking like you. There are a few things I can stomach less than traitors. I rank them damn near down there with child molesters."

Tolley stabbed a finger at the satellite imagery. The buildings were marked A, B and so on. "Your guys in that Spectre better lay on some precision firing. I'm talking bull's-eye right out of the gate. You've got about a two-hundred-yard clearance from the tents."

"They'll get it done."

"No margin for error."

"I understand."

"So, we go in and mop up what's left?"

"That's how it's going to work."

"Captain Parker and Colonel Morton. Those are the big fish in charge. U.S. Special Forces, Vietnam, Panama, the Gulf. They're your link to the Pentagon brass and on down to the NSA, and few more of those snakes."

Bolan had been provided the intel packages on the two traitors by the Farm. He couldn't help but wonder where it had gone wrong for the two soldiers, but he wasn't going in to psychoanalyze them.

They were history, unless they hit their knees before him, empty hands in the air.

Fat chance.

"One more time? You want me to go over the pics again?"

Bolan shook his head. Maybe Tolley was just suffering from a case of precombat jitters and needed to talk. The soldier already had the lay of the compound. It was spread out in a jungle clearing, roughly two football fields, mock-ups, barracks, armory, with six main trails branching off to the north and east. The runway was long enough for the Spectre to land once the ground force had the compound cleared. According to satellite monitoring, maybe half of the men—the real soldiers—were the only ones who appeared constantly armed. Grimaldi was ordered to just take out the aircraft, Humvees and the two main barracks. Using the Spectre might prove a little more firepower than necessary, overkill in fact, but Grimaldi had been thinking ahead to North Korea. A large military installation where the sub would eventually dock had been marked by satellite recon.

Later, but it couldn't come soon enough. The soldier didn't want to get ahead of himself.

"You're with me and my team," Bolan told Tolley. "I want that stash site secured, first off, if possible."

"Well, the commander and the colonel. I don't think they're going to want to go quietly. Know what I mean. They may want to light us up when it hits the fan."

"I'm not here to ask them nicely to surrender."

Tolley nodded. "I've seen you work. For some reason, I believe that."

7

Jack Morton was feeling mean and desperate. If living well was the best revenge, the former United States Special Forces colonel thought, Papua New Guinea wasn't going to be his ticket to paradise.

Far from it.

There were problems everywhere—like about a hundred-plus right before his eyes—and he wasn't sure where it all went next. Not only that, but there had been no messenger service, no supply drops, no communication from the States to fill him in on their plans. Just another load of bums, flown in by the council, he was supposed to whip into combat shape. What the hell, he figured they expected him to perform miracles. The problem was he'd been paid a quarter million up front to land there eighteen months ago to do the council's bidding.

Make soldiers out of civilians.

Well, he wasn't running a detox center, by God, but the generals seemed hell-bent on continuing to send him bums, burnouts, drunks, drug addicts and petty criminals. Since he had no direct line to Washington, he was in the dark these days about whatever their plans. In the beginning the idea was to stick to bona fide ex-military types, real soldiers with combat experience, down on their luck, yes, but hungry to show themselves as warriors again. Then again, he thought, drawing on his cigarette as he walked down the trail away from his command hut, what was their master plan? About all he knew on that score was ten cities had been chosen for attack, to be held hostage by weapons of mass destruction until the generals delivered their terms to the White House. But when? What cities? How much longer could he endure this steaming backwater hellhole?

What could he do? He was there, stuck in PNG, land of headhunters, ex-pats and mercenaries, where the power structure out of Moresby was as corrupt as any he'd ever seen anywhere. And the generals were in D.C., sitting silently in their Pentagon abode, while the Phoenix Council was God only knew where.

Leaving him to sweat it out.

His stomach was getting worse these days, too, all knotted up. Some days his bowels were a quaking mess, rendering him unable to eat what was shipped in from Port Moresby, thus confined to small intakes of bottled water. He couldn't sleep, couldn't eat. Maybe it was all the responsibility of running a training camp—and he nearly laughed out loud at the notion that that's what this slice of hell on earth slashed out of the jungle was—getting on his nerves. Fifty real soldiers, fifty bums packed together along the trail. He understood the concept of cannon fodder, but he was dubious, even with the promise of a cash incentive, that the bum squads would hold up their end when the time came—whenever that was.

He kept walking up the winding path, listening to the howls and caws of wildlife, the mosquitoes mercifully leaving him alone as he hung a halo of smoke over his head. He checked the ridge of the volcanic plateau and found Serville watching the broken land that rolled and jutted and dropped in gullies ripped out by earthquakes to the south, away from camp. Worried, he guessed about Dunas or Daroa tribesmen skulking up on him out of the night. The closest tribe was several miles up the river, and Morton kept them happy with a case of whiskey and cold cash. One trip a month to keep them quiet and away from camp, giving them all the privacy they needed. Same thing for the big shots in Port Moresby, only they wanted money more than a whiskey buzz.

He checked the murky light of predawn, walking on, spotting the six other sentries wandering the perimeter, armed with assault rifles, and God help them, he thought, if they nodded off on the job. Whatever was riding on the line, well, he could ill afford to see the special merchandise stashed in his hut vanish off into the jungle. He worried about attack all the time, but it wouldn't rear up from the natives. He kept thinking someone in Washington would uncover the plot, someone breaking down, talking, aiming a black-ops team his way. A hundred-plus men, half of whom stayed armed even while they slept, and he thought the notion of a surgical strike against him a little out of the realm of possibility. Nothing short of a full strike, air fire support and ground troops, could possibly do the job.

Morton was in the act of lighting another cigarette when he heard a familiar sound. One that disturbed him greatly.

He stopped cold, the bleat of chopper blades growing from the south. What the hell was this?

Serville patched through, panic clear in his voice as he said, "Colonel, we've got a problem."

He was his on radio, listening to Serville report that a Sea Stallion—a frigging Navy chopper—was unloading a dozen armed men, when the cigarette fell from his lip. If he thought he had problems and worries before, he was thinking their little gig in the jungle had been found out.

And his whole world was about to come crashing down, his worst nightmare realized.

THE DOOMSDAY ARMY was damned as far as Bolan was concerned. These men were traitors, selling out their country and their souls in the name of money and twisted ideology. Brognola had confirmed more of what Tolley had laid out about the recruiting angle of the Phoenix Council. A number of the enemy were indeed former soldiers, but the other half, it seemed, were pretty much common criminals desperate for quick money. The Executioner, along with Alpha Teams One and Two, would lay waste to the place.

With, of course, a little help from the Spectre.

The soldier led the charge, running down a wide gash in the plateau, carved out by Mother Nature, taking the path of least resistance as mapped out by satellite imagery. He'd sighted the lone sentry on the ridge to the north, and it was Alpha Two's job to take him out and to secure the airfield beyond. Once this was wrapped, Bolan intended to use the place, or whatever was left standing, as a temporary base of operations.

There were a few snakes in Port Moresby he needed to call upon also.

Then there was the not so little matter of Colonel Chongjin and a foray into North Korea.

One nest of vipers at a time. This wasn't going to be easy, no matter how it was sliced and diced from the initial blast of death from above.

The Spectre was already rumbling in from the south, ready to lower the boom. With Tolley beside him, Alpha One running in a skirmish line, Bolan raised his M-16 as the two sentries rolled around the tree line at the south edge of the camp.

The Executioner, along with his troops, fired off a concentrated burst of autofire, nailing the two guards and got the war in the jungle jump-started.

RUPERT HADLEY HAD to leave before the nightmare grew worse. He hadn't slept a wink all night, tossing and turning in his bunk. Visions of the crocodile were branded in his mind. Another two feet farther out in the water and that would have been him getting chomped in half, dragged under and consumed in bloody chunks. No, he couldn't take it anymore.

He was leaving this hellhole.

But how? Slip out the back of the tent, tell a roving sentry he needed to take a leak maybe. Then make a mad dash for one of the Humvees and hope to God keys were in the ignition. Then what? He didn't even know what country he was in. Well, anything was better than grunting and sweating out twelve hours a day in physical training, washing himself off in crocodile-infested waters, soiling himself out of terror and forced to lie in his own filth.

He got out of his bunk and looked around for watching eyes. Everyone appeared to be asleep, too exhausted by the day's heat, fighting mosquitoes and running around twelve to fifteen hours, he reckoned.

Time to bolt. He'd find a way out. He had to. He wasn't dying in an unknown land, humiliated on a daily basis, not knowing why he was even there to maybe die for whatever reason, from whatever source of horror. For all he knew, poisonous snakes and spiders could be creeping around the tent that very second.

He padded to the deepest back corner of the tent, lowering himself, looking back over his shoulder. So far so good. Deep snores sounding off everywhere, but no whispering at him or guys waking, wondering what the hell he was doing. He was squeezing himself through the edge at the bottom of the tent when the shooting erupted.

Voices were raised in alarm all over the camp. What the hell? They were under attack.

Who? Why?

No matter. His heart was racing. he was figuring this was his lucky break, a diversion he could use to steal a vehicle, then he heard what sounded like the greatest peals of thunder he could have ever imagined, a sound like the end of the world.

Then the whole tent blew up in great balls of fire and choking smoke. A shock wave lifted him up and carried him away, clear of the raging firestorm behind him.

MORTON WAS RACING toward the larger troop tent, yelling for guys to get it in gear on the double, a few of them already through the flap with assault rifles, when he heard the rolling thunder. The colonel turned and saw the behemoth flying battleship cruising in low from the south, nearly hugging the tree line, then he made out the cannons on the port side and knew they were all a done deal.

That was an AC-130 Spectre gunship, he knew, since he'd been aboard one during the Panama invasion when they went to snatch Noriega. Big firepower. Earth-eating doom from above, in fact. So they were found out, a black operation was in his face, someone coming to wax them all.

He hit the ground, unable to think of anything else to do when the world erupted in hellish thunder all around, a pounding that seemed to carve him up from head to toe. He thought the earth would open up and swallow him, but he held on, thinking any second he'd be blown all over the jungle. Somehow he summoned the courage to look up, deciding if he was going to die that second, he'd stare death in the face.

It didn't happen to him, but both tents were thrashed to shreds by the pounding cannonfire. Bits and pieces of wet things slapped him in the face—body parts, he was sure. The scorching heat of screaming fire reached out for him, a scalding wave that singed his eyeballs.

He flinched as a severed leg banged off the top of his head.

The screams started next, men amputated, no doubt, or set ablaze. Ride it out, he thought, running for his hut to grab a weapon. The least he could do was die on his feet, fighting.

THE EXECUTIONER HELD up Alpha One long enough to let Grimaldi and company bludgeon the camp. It was a fearsome sight to behold, Bolan and troops fanning out, grabbing cover behind the line of fat trees and tangled foliage, watching it happen. Everything was chopped and churned by the combined firepower of the Spectre. The massive warbird seemed to damn near skim the camp, sailing on, slowly raining down its scourge. They threw the works at the camp, everything from the 105 mm howitzer, the two 20 mm Vulcan Gatling cannons and the Bofors.

Despite the bombardment survivors staggered into view.

"Let's rock and rip," the Executioner told his troops, breaking the camp perimeter, going in, already lining up targets.

HADLEY WAS SURE he was dead, his body feeling beaten by a baseball bat. Well, if he was in that much pain, he was still breathing. So what happened? Thrown clear of the blast, landing somewhere in dense brush, he figured, a human ball tossed about by the explosion. And what was happening now?

He saw them, black wraiths, armed with assault rifles, wading right into the camp, shooting up the place. He didn't care who they were as long as they didn't spot him. He hid, thinking he could use all the billowing waves of smoke as a shield. He needed to get to a Humvee somehow and get the hell out of there.

Whoever these guys in blacksuits and war paint were, they were showing no mercy. There were men with no arms getting dropped by autofire. Other figures staggered out of the tent ruins, some triggering assault rifles but getting nailed in the process.

He stood as the shadow killers kept moving past. He smelled the air, nearly retched as he whiffed all the blood and emptied bowels and whatever else had gotten chewed up by the bombardment. What had hit them? And what did it matter now?

He began his own march into the jungle, ignoring the vines tearing at his face, his eyelids cracked to slits.

The shooting went on and on. It was a horror show out there beyond the smoke and fire, and he needed to make himself as scarce as possible and vacate. They weren't taking prisoners. It occurred to him this place was some sort of mercenary camp and they had been branded by their attackers as criminals destined only for execution.

Hadley kept moving, trying to control his wheezing as he crashed through the brush.

8

If the crew members of the Spectre were on his team, Morton would have stood and saluted that bunch of seasoned killers from above. As it stood, he could only curse them, gnash his teeth and briefly wonder how in the world it had all come down to this.

Of course, they knew the layout, the camp proper and beyond, what was what and who was where, thanks to either someone's loose traitorous lips or satellite imagery or both, he damn well suspected. Even still, they hit exactly what they wanted, down to the yard, a precision bombardment that had left nothing but smoking craters where the troop barracks had stood and bodies and body parts strewed from there to the airfield and down to the river. Of course, no amount of bombing by even laser-guided missiles on a given target ever nailed every last building.

Wait a second, Morton thought, hauling himself toward his command hut. It was still standing. And how about that? Coincidence? He didn't think so.

He grabbed up a discarded MP-5 from the nearest corpse, checked the clip and slapped it home, cocked and locked. Bodies, some bloodied, some screaming like the damned, some missing an arm or crawling along minus a leg, looked to make up a nice wall of flesh, a momentary blockade or some combatant maze for the hitters, buying him time to attempt the idea shaping up in his head. Yes, the Spectre had sailed on when it could have easily taken out his command post. Why? Well, the answer was obvious in his mind. Whoever had blabbed about the camp also knew where the merchandise was housed. That meant the flyboys were under orders not to lower the hammer on his hut and risk contaminating their own people with clouds of viral poison, nerve gas and leaking radiation. And the hitters weren't coming in, burdened by HAZMAT space suits. They were coming to preserve and take the big stuff for themselves—as well as wax everybody in camp.

Maybe he had a chance to save himself, he decided, checking the killing ground behind him. A wave of staggering men was getting eaten all to hell by the mystery force, their bodies absorbing bullets that might have otherwise found his tail.

Twelve packages in all, still intact, he knew. It would take too long to work the digital computer combination on any of the four nuke backpacks, but the aluminum suitcases were rigged with explosives, ready to erupt poison. All he needed to do was release the primer catch on the suitcase, and bang. If he was going down he wouldn't go alone. Hell, he take all of PNG if he had to.

One chance, a big, fat gamble, staving off his own death any way he could. He'd grab a Humvee or better still a chopper—if one of his pilots was still in one piece. Then make Port Moresby, where any number of expat, merc goons and corrupt power players who had taken his cash for their deaf, dumb and blind routine would get him safely the hell out of Papua New Guinea.

He had to try, nothing else to do, unless he wanted to stay there and get cut to ribbons. He pumped his legs and braced for the bullet that would find his flesh, send him pitching on his way out of there.

Morton made the door of his command post, free and clear. The racket of weapons fire sounded like the scourge of hell at his back as he and barreled for the stash hole.

IT WAS TAG and leave them where they dropped. They were scattering in different directions, but Bolan and his Alpha teams had them covered, sighted and pretty much nailed. All that was left to do was hunt them down and pull the trigger. The soldier, Tolley and his blacksuits kept moving in, mopping up. Whether they ran, held their ground and fought, came moaning or even crawling, bloodied and mauled out of the smoke and flames, they were fair game. Those were Bolan's orders. No mercy, no prisoners unless they begged for capture.

No takers for pity or captivity turned up. Whether it was shock or fight or flight that spurred the enemy on, it made no difference to Bolan. It was just as well, as far as he was concerned. These men were a scourge, a wheel in the cog of the Phoenix Council's conspiracy. They had made their choice long ago.

Time to pony up.

The Executioner and his team were spaced well apart, no easy spray and pray that would nail them. The shreds of floating canvas rained down, obscuring some fields of fire for the soldier. But the edge of the jungle was on fire now, as the few kerosene lamps lighting the camp had dispersed like hungry torches during the Spectre's bombardment. Whatever had been in the fuel bins had also been ignited into a lake of fire. The enemy was lit up. Glowing bull's-eyes.

Marching, they sealed most of the runners and the wounded off in a pincers assault. Bolan had the spearhead, Tolley next to him. They kept rolling on, taking all targets beyond the boiling smoke and walls of fire. Mercy shots were pumped into the wounded, and Bolan took a quick count of shadows scurrying about.

Down to fifteen, twenty tops. Still a problem, since most of them were armed and headed for the airfield. Out there, Alpha Two wasted no time eliminating the lone sentry. There was ammo and hellbombs to spare, so one of the blacksuits simply blew the sentry off the ridge with a 40 mm round. Alpha Two started coming down the ridge on a shooting intercept line.

One armed shadow in particular grabbed Bolan's attention next. He couldn't say exactly who it was, but he was banking it was one of the camp's so-called officers. The man was hell-bent on hauling ass for the one structure Bolan knew Grimaldi and company wouldn't take out.

The command post was at the end of the trail and that was where the packages were stored. The soldier envisioned some suicide stand coming.

Bolan was breaking through a wall of smoke, shooting up two shadows near the tree line, when a figure suddenly darted out of the jungle and barreled into a Humvee.

FEAR AND INSTINCT seized Hadley. He didn't know anymore what he was doing, how he did it, but he made the Humvee. With the engine fired up he was lurching

ahead. Dumb luck or fate, he didn't care, he was at the
wheel. It was an escalating nightmare everywhere he
looked, and he really didn't care to take it in. Dead guys
everywhere. Wounded getting no special treatment, just
sponging a quick burst of autofire, down and out.

Straight ahead, nothing but a bull charge, he thought.
There was some open ground, but not much clearance
down there past all that swirling fire. And then there was
the army of death, too busy blasting away and dropping
guys to be concerned about him.

He was putting pedal to the metal, surging ahead,
thinking a few more seconds and he was on his way
when he saw it.

What the hell? The big shadow came out of nowhere,
walking right out of the smoke and fire like he was a living part of it, or owned it like some shroud. Hadley was
cutting the distance, lowering his head beneath the steering column, sure the windshield was about to get blown
in his face, when he glimpsed the tubelike object fixed
to the assault rifle. No muzzle-flashes winking, but he
thought there was and flame blossomed from the tube,
something zigzagging through the air, locked onto his
charge like a magnet.

His mind told him what it was—and he screamed.

BOLAN WASN'T TAKING any chances or wasting one second disposing of any runners. The Humvee was racing
right at him, the wheelman shaving the distance fast and
hard when the soldier tapped the M-203's trigger. The
missile sailed on, a face of horror lit up inside the vehicle by the dancing flames nearby, then the impact

fuse detonated against the windshield. The blast sheared the Humvee apart like a flimsy tin can.

A quick scouting of the action, wreckage winging back down the trail, and Bolan could sense it winding down to a few stragglers. Alpha Two was pummeling any would-be pilots with blazing autofire and two 40 mm blasts. For the enemy, it was all over but the dying.

The Executioner cracked home a fresh clip in his assault rifle, scanning the edge of the jungle. Two shadows were making tracks down the trail leading for the river when the warrior drilled them off their feet with two quick bursts to the back.

The Executioner set his sights on the command post, and heard the voice bellow out from the doorway, "Hey, this is Colonel Morton! I'm walking out of here, and I'll tell you why! I suggest you hold your fire and listen real good!"

THE BIG GUY MOVED like a pro who had done this sort of killing a thousand times, but Morton wasn't surprised by what he found. There was something in his eyes, as the guy kept marching slowly down the trail, heading his way. A look that warned Morton whatever he was about to try and sell wasn't going to work.

Well, he'd come this far, so he stepped out of the hut. Time to walk or fall.

It was awkward, waving the subgun around, one eye on the killzone out on the airfield, while holding on to the case, but it wouldn't take but a second to slide his thumb over the detonating button. Morton moved to the side, watching the big guy.

"One more step and we're all history, mister!"

"It's all over. Time to give it up."

"I don't think so. With this baby I'm holding, all I have to do is punch a little button and I'll release a nice little cloud of nerve gas. Well, I don't see any space suits around. Getting the picture?"

Morton chuckled. The big guy had stopped moving.

"I see I have your attention."

THE EXECUTIONER WEIGHED the odds against a quick burst to the guy's head. He felt the sudden jackhammer that was his heart. He had no doubt the enemy would commit suicide and take all of them with him.

"What! No deal for me? I can give you plenty of names, especially the boys in Port Moresby who helped set up and watch my little candy store."

Bolan knew he'd have to go for it, just as soon as those eyes flickered away. He steeled himself to bring up the M-16, then a shot rang out, a dark tuft of the enemy's skull flying away.

The body toppled, Bolan feeling his heart lurch, but there was no explosion. He looked down the line and found Tolley lowering his M-16.

"I'm sure you were thinking the same thing," Tolley said.

Bolan nodded, sized up the shooting war out on the airfield. There were sporadic bursts of autofire as Alpha Two closed in on the few survivors desperately trying to make the Huey. When the last shadow fell, the Executioner plucked his tac radio off his belt to bring Grimaldi in.

THE HAZMAT TEAM WAS bringing out the cases and the nuke backpacks as Bolan took a long stroll around the airfield, then searched briefly through the jungle of the camp perimeter for any man who might have escaped or lay wounded.

Nothing but the dead.

The Spectre had landed, barely making the three thousand feet of runway available to the north. Bolan congratulated Grimaldi and company on a job well done and asked his friend to ring up Brognola on the sat link for an update. He shuddered to think what would have happened if one of Spectre's rounds had uprooted the command hut.

He caught himself. It was done, but there was still plenty left to do.

He suddenly wondered how many had died there? For what? Why? Soldiers who had taken an oath to defend and protect their country instead became traitors. The worst of savages in Bolan's mind. Impossible to take a body count and Bolan reckoned he didn't much care to. They were all dead.

He could feel Tolley watching him as he took in the space suits carefully loading up the backpacks and the aluminum cases in lead containers, settling them into foam cushioning. From there, they would be rolled onto the gunship. Bolan would let Brognola decide where to take them next.

The soldier again took in the carnage, weighing and feeling the enormity of the past few days. Since New York he had hunted down terrorists, black-ops assassins, every ilk of traitor and scumbag that the Phoenix Council had called upon, recruited or extorted to its twisted cause. Hundreds of American citizens had been mur-

dered or wounded since a lone Iraqi gunman had opened
fire on a subway train in Manhattan. Riots had erupted
in certain cities, out of fear and panic. He wondered
where would it go from there? Well, Bolan had some
ideas and they involved the power players who had covered for the Doomsday Army.

Bolan glanced at Tolley. "You did good."

Tolley showed a mean grin. "I'm dismissed."

"Not yet."

"Sounds like you've got something in mind."

"I do. This might be the most isolated and uninhab-
ited part of PNG, but somebody let these guys in the
door."

Tolley nodded. "I know who they are and where they
are."

It was Bolan's turn to crack a grin.

"Uh-huh. Wondering how come I know so much? I
told you, I was let in, all the way."

"They trusted you that much?"

"What can I say? They did. Obviously that was their
mistake. You wondering maybe if you can trust me?"

"If I didn't by now, you wouldn't be standing here."

"Fair enough," Tolley stated. "I also know those suitcases packed with nerve gas and very nasty genetically-
engineered anthrax and botulism came from a classified
base in Nevada. I know the black-ops men who over-
saw the operation are still there. They get instructions
and payoffs at a specific location. I even have the ac-
cess number to their secured line. One call and I know
where I can set them up for a rendezvous."

"I'll need specifics, but that's later."

"So, what now?"

"I need to talk to Albert," Bolan said, referring to Brognola.

"You've got unfinished business here in PNG?"

"I'll need you to point the way. No sense in leaving the guilty unpunished."

"None at all. The bastards who covered for these guys are just as guilty in my mind."

"I can't argue with that," Bolan said, then turned and marched for the Spectre.

9

"How come I smell something fishy where that guy's concerned?" Bolan asked Brognola when he heard what the big Fed informed him over the sat link.

The Executioner was near the cargo hold in the gunship, Tolley and Grimaldi by his side. The containers with their doomsday payloads were in the bay area. The HAZMAT specialists were fastening them to the bulkhead by thick canvas webbing.

"I admit it's extremely unusual," Brognola said. "But that's what I'm hearing from the Man."

"Let me get this straight," Bolan said. "Kim Jong Il called the White House, full of apologies for his renegade Colonel Chongjin. Said we're welcome to come and get him and what Kim Jong's calling an outlaw army in Haeju."

"That's the gist of it, Striker. He even told our people where the sub will be docking, but we already knew that. We've got satellites parked in space watching the area in question. Our ASW teams tell us at the speed the sub is going they'll pull in sometime tonight. By then the USS *Enterprise* will have come within range in the Yellow Sea for it to send out its fighters."

"And we're still in the game?"

"The Man wants you and our people to go in as the ground force. We'll have to work out the logistics and timing between the fighters and the ground troops, but the Man's says you've gone this far, and he's damn pleased with progress."

"Our fighters can bomb the hell out of this military complex where the captives will be held."

"That's the general idea. Antiaircraft batteries, bivouacs, their own fighter jets, like that. We're poring over sat imagery now, nailing down what's what. At first look, I'd say it's a big base, two dozen buildings, an airfield nearby, then there's a nuclear reactor, what looks like a factory. Maybe a hundred or more North Korean soldiers we're dealing with."

"Four of my people are out of the game. They were hit, but I'm told they're stabilized and they'll make it. They're on the Sea Stallion now heading out."

"I'll make the arrangements to get them home. But I don't think I can spare any more of our guys."

"I'll go with what I have."

"If Grimaldi and crew can do the same bang-up job on this installation as they did there, well, it'll be up to you and the others to go in, mop up and extract those hostages. Of course, they'll go in behind our fighters, take out what's left, if that's how the air strike goes down. There are fifteen hostages Chongjin's holding on to, according to my sources. I'll send the names and faces over the fax so you know who you're looking for."

"What I don't understand is why the change of heart on Kim Jong's part?"

"He's a nutcase. I guess he's nervous about a full-scale invasion. He got cold feet, figured in a sober moment it's gone too far."

"Okay, I've got maybe six or seven hours to wrap things up here."

"You're going after this Wiggins and the other high rollers? I don't know, Striker. We've got a CIA base on an island near the DMZ where we can set you up to go. It's going to be shaving it all close, might even leave you out of it."

"No sense in leaving behind unfinished business. And then there's that list of conspirators of Tolley's you combed through."

"A long and very ugly one at that."

"I'm thinking by the time I clean it up here, you'll have the details ironed out."

"I know that tone and I guess there's no changing your mind."

"No. It's time to turn up the heat, scorched earth from here on. Tolley says he can point the way. Okay? The fuel bladders were spared, so we can gas up here and get to this CIA base after I wrap it up here on PNG."

"You'll have everything you'll need there to get the job done on Chongjin. By the way, not that I don't trust what I've got so far from Tolley, but we've got CIA on PNG and they've confirmed this Sir Charles Wiggins and a few others seem to stay holed up these days at his beachfront compound. I'll send the details along pronto."

"Do it."

"I'M TELLING YOU, I saw two men!"

"Then get up there and take Kirkland with you."

Roger Stallins was an American expatriate, ten years out of the United States Army, with stints as a mercenary and gunrunner along the way in Southeast Asia. The heat was turned up by the authorities in Thailand two years back, following a bust by the DEA, and PNG sounded as good a place as any to hide out and find work. Thief, dope dealer, gambler, it didn't matter as long as he stayed active and out there on the edge.

The problem was he wasn't working or at least didn't consider his assignment—head of security for Sir Charles Wiggins—as gainful employment. Sure, the great man in the white jacket paid him, but he was little more than butler, it seemed, these days. Sure, he was armed with an Uzi and controlled ten men, most of them Aussie mercs, but he could see no enemies of the man of the estate on this lush island compound. Naturally, he thought, Wiggins saw bogeymen everywhere he looked and was constantly harping about security. It was the Americans up the Fly River that had him jumping at shadows lately. In fact, the moneymen who'd given sanctuary to the American army were gathered under the roof, three days running of paranoid talk. Bankers, bagmen, politicians were worried maybe the real source of their income would get flushed out of the dark.

Action or no action, Stallings didn't think he'd last much longer, spending long days strolling around the grounds, checking for armed shadows in the trees, the garage or down the beach since he'd always considered himself a man who needed action.

Something was happening up the tree-blanketed slope. He heard the chopper himself, which had brought him outside, down the pool deck, staring over the corral rock wall up the slope. He had given the order for the Aussies to go check out their own bogeymen, but they looked reluctant to move out. Maybe it was the fact they were taking orders from an American, but Wiggins had put him in charge. They didn't have to like it; they just had to obey.

"What are you waiting for?"

They exchanged scowls, but were moving up the trail when two shots cracked through the morning air. The curse was leaping out of Stallings's mouth just as the two Aussies toppled, their skulls shattered and leaking blood and gore.

It occurred to Stallings that maybe Wiggins had good reason to be paranoid after all.

THE EXECUTIONER WAS on the clock, and there was no point wasting time. They'd done a brief recon from above the jagged black volcanic ridgeline to the north, Grimaldi at the helm of the Huey gunship.

It was a two-story whitewashed stone mansion, palm trees and pool. The motor pool was to the east, six vehicles in all, including SUVs, a Cadillac and a Mercedes. As far as he could see, Tolley's and Brognola's sources had been right. The moneymen were gathered, worried about their world falling apart, no doubt. The armed sentries patrolling the grounds struck Bolan as grizzled merc types, who were shaggy and unshaven but carrying Uzis. Bankers, politicians and bagmen for the

Australian Defence Cooperation Program. In Bolan's mind, they were every bit as dirty and guilty as the main viper's nest of conspirators of the Phoenix Council. Maybe worse, since by giving the Doomsday Army refuge in the jungle, they aided and abetted those who were planning to launch yet more attacks against American citizens.

Two killing shots got it started. Bolan and Tolley tagged the two hardmen outside the corral rock pool wall. It was Tolley's task to make the motor pool while Bolan crashed the French doors in the back. They would run for the motor pool unless he missed his guess. There was nowhere to run.

Tolley slashed a hard run to Bolan's left flank while the soldier advanced straight ahead for the pool area. The merc in charge was on his handheld radio, barking up a storm as soon as he watched his two men drop. Bolan rolled out from between the palm trees, tapped the M-16's trigger and ripped a burst over the man's chest, sending him dancing back, Uzi and radio flying as he windmilled his arms and splashed down in the pool.

The Executioner vaulted the wall. They came running out the French doors, four hardmen gaping around, surprise in their eyes. No point in delaying the inevitable, so the soldier squeezed the M-203's trigger. The blast sent them screaming and flying back into the doors. By now the Executioner could be sure, even at the early hour, everyone under the roof was wide awake.

Bolan charged into the churning smoke, searching for fresh targets.

TOLLEY HURLED a frag grenade as the first wave came barreling around the corner of the garage. Some were in suit jackets, flapping their hands, squawking out their fear. Some were armed, and as soon as the steel egg was sailing and rolling up beneath the Caddie, Tolley hosed down three hardmen with a stitching burst across their torsos, sending them crashing into the men in suits. The grenade blew, lifting the Caddie into the air.

Tolley was far from finished wrecking the motor pool. In fact, Belasko said to wipe it all out.

With pleasure.

Taking cover behind a palm tree, Tolley began pumping out one 40 mm round after another. They were running back through the garage now, thinking they might be safe inside the house.

Bad move.

They were retreating right back to their deaths.

It didn't take more than twelve seconds tops, but Tolley had the motor pool blown to fiery scrap.

No way out.

Just as Belasko wanted.

"WHO THE HELL are you?"

The man in the white coat was committed to Bolan's memory from the intel package sent along by Brognola.

Sir Charles Wiggins. He came from old family money, his father and his father's father having made their fortune in gold and silver as a supposed arm of Bougainville Ltd. Apparently their rise to the top had been guaranteed by a mercenary army, extortion and plain ruthlessness. Later on they bought up influence, controlling the political structure, top to bottom in Papua New Guinea, all the way to the Australian military. The son wasn't much more than a greedy playboy, according to the intel, but at the moment he was armed with a pistol and was standing in the middle of his lavish living room.

Bolan advanced, then heard the thunder of Tolley's work, the walls shaking as the man took care of any immediate hope of evacuation.

"Colonel Morton is finished."

The Executioner could have told the dark-haired man to lose the piece, give it up and come quietly. After tracking the conspirators halfway around the world, after all the Americans who had been murdered by the Phoenix Council's terrorist lackeys, the soldier wasn't in any mood to bargain or hand out the hope of immunity.

No more. From there on, he was cranking up the heat, taking them all down, armed or not. If they were dirty, they were done.

"What?"

"He didn't make it. You're not going to, either," Bolan stated.

"Look, we can deal."

"You have nothing to offer."

"There's a half million in cash at the old Port Moresby Hotel."

Bolan played as though he was interested. The

money was news to him, but the hotel was next on his hit list anyway.

"I'm listening."

"American and Aussie mercs. They have the top floor to themselves, a suite. They're bagmen for the Australian Defence Cooperation Program. They're supposed to be leaving sometime today."

"Payoff money?"

"Right. Maybe I can cut you in for a piece of the action."

Bolan nodded. He looked around the living room. Oil paintings, couches, divans and other antique furniture from the old colonial days. Old-world money. A swank mansion on the beach, Wiggins looking to bargain to hold on to the good life.

"I'm afraid all the money in the world won't buy me out, Wiggins."

"Are you telling me I'm finished? Are you going to make me give up all of this."

Bolan made a show of looking down the hall as he heard the racket of pounding feet coming from that direction.

And Wiggins went for it, the pistol sweeping up, the man hoping one lucky shot would save his kingdom.

The M-16 was already rising, spitting lead and chopping the man's white coat to crimson ruins.

The Executioner was rounding the corner of the archway at the end of the living room when they came running down the adjacent hallway.

At the sight of the big man with the M-16, they were skidding to a halt, eyes going wide, men bumping into each other. Two were lugging Uzis, but a few of the suits had opted to arm themselves with pistols.

The Executioner held back on the trigger of his assault rifle and swept a blistering salvo down the line.

They were pitching into the walls, flayed to crimson rags, all screams and twitching arms. A few of them tried to bolt, but Bolan spotted Tolley making his backdoor entrance. Caught in the cross fire, the moneymen were scythed and diced, dancing out the final jig.

When the last one dropped, Bolan changed clips.

"Let's take a walk through the place and see if anybody chose to hide under the bed," the Executioner told Tolley.

10

The black bag was all Jack Wilson could think about. It had been a long night, tossing and turning on the divan, men wandering about in the suite, drinking, yukking it up, playing poker. But even with his eyes shut, late at night, Wilson felt them all around him, gruff and grim, making him wonder if they weren't thinking the same thing he was.

The bag.

There was little doubt in his mind that they were every bit as hungry about it as he was, probably seething at the very idea they'd have to hand it over.

It was perched at the end of the bar, bulging with five hundred large—and in American dollars not the worthless kina of PNG. And where was it going? he thought. Some Aussie mucka-mucks were supposedly flying in that morning, ready to scoop it up, take it back to Sydney and spread the loot around.

Payoff cash.

Wilson sat up, rubbing his eyes, feeling like crap on a stick since he hadn't slept a wink, his brain a puddle of sludge from all the booze he'd sucked down the past night at the Old Bum's Tavern.

There were twelve of them in the sprawling suite, but the Uzis, AKs, Ingrams and holstered Glocks spoke volumes to him about what would happen if somebody—inside or outside the room—had any peculiar notions about getting rich on the spot.

Wilson looked to the curtained windows. The sun was up, and coupled with all the noise of the natives hawking wares and tourists and whoever else going to market at that ungodly hour, it was like a knife through his jellied brain, making him wince, bringing on the bile. Just another day guarding the store while others got rich, he brooded. He wondered why, with all the money getting passed around, they couldn't be holed up in posher digs. There were Ela and Koki Beaches, with any number of hotels where fat-cat tourists and expats with bucks to burn lounged in the bars all night, a whore on each arm, then maybe hit the beach during the day to work on the piña coladas and their tan. It didn't make sense, sitting in some room, big as it was, complete with bar, but with the paint peeling off the walls, three of those ceiling fans—which constantly squeaked and rattled as if they were ready to drop—the only thing that kept the hot air moving. And Hanuabada wasn't exactly paradise, mapped out in somebody's tour guide, starred as a sight to behold and brag to the grandkids about in their twilight years. There were more thieves, pickpockets, drunks, all manner of petty criminals, expats and mercs down on their luck lurking this part of town. It was barely safe enough for a man armed to the teeth to move about during the day. Not even the cops showed their faces around there unless it was to pick up a fat envelope. But that was Port Moresby. Everybody had his or her hand out, always hunting down a particular vision of heaven on earth.

Well, there was no paradise for Wilson, never had been and probably never would be. Where had it all gone wrong for him? he wondered, stifling a groan. He had failed at everything in life he had attempted. Sectioned-Eight out of the Army, drifting aimlessly from job to job through the Southwest. Failed marriage, two kids, the ex-wife demanding money all the time. Which, he reasoned, had driven him to commit a string of armed robberies. Liquor stores, grocery stores, gas stations. The old desert rat behind the counter outside Tucson had changed his life forever, and it was pretty much because he'd been forced to saw the guy in half with a shotgun, the old buzzard thinking he was Clint Eastwood or something with his Magnum.

Well, he had to admit to himself he wasn't a complete dismal failure.

Wilson had made *America's Most Wanted*. He was a TV star.

And that in turn had sent him flying out of the country, one step ahead of the law. From there he'd somehow made it to Sydney, where he'd run into two old Army buddies who were just about as down on their luck as he was. Only it seemed they knew people up north in Port Moresby. Guys, mostly Aussies, who could use their particular martial skills, or so his buddies had claimed after a few belts at the local pub.

So there he was. One thing had led to another, his life little more than a crapshoot. Three years in PNG, guarding the roost, making sure the big shots about town got from point A to B.

Hell, he was little more than a glorified gopher.

The Ingram MAC-10 was at his feet. He gave it a glance, checking out his surroundings, thinking dark thoughts and weighing his chances.

There were only so many beds, couches, and several of the Aussies had brought in cots. They were still snoring in corners of the room, but it was the big man slumped back in the leather recliner near the bar who concerned him the most. Crofton never let go of the 12-gauge riot gun. It was resting across his lap. The hatchet-faced guy was broad in the shoulders, tapered down the other way, like the reverse of some of the volcanoes Wilson had seen near the city. Just looking at the man made him nervous.

What a life, he thought, rising, flinching at the sound of bones cracking in his knees. Why had the brass ring always eluded him?

If he could just get his hands on that bag. Then what? Blast them all? Bolt out the door, buy his way out of PNG?

He wasn't aware he'd slung the compact subgun around his shoulder until he was at the bar.

"Something I can do for you, mate?"

He was reaching for a bottle of whiskey, his hands shaking, when he jumped at the voice. He turned his head, mouth open, finding Crofton in the same leaned-back position, a piece of stone. Hell, the man hadn't even opened his eyes. It was as if he sensed him standing there.

Spooky. Or maybe he'd heard his joints creaking and snapping, or maybe his nose was tuned into all the boozy sweat running down Wilson's face, soaking his shirt.

"Just need something for the shakes."

Crofton grunted.

And that noncommittal response shot the tremors even worse through his hands.

He killed a deep slug, the warmth spreading through his belly. He felt better in a few moments, head clearing, some iron back in the legs. He resisted the urge to look at the bag, sure the Aussie was watching him through the merest slit in his eyelids. Bottle in hand, he was shuffling back for the divan when he nearly screamed at the blast of noise that bowled him off his feet.

And suddenly everyone in the room was up and moving for the windows, weapons in hand. He was sure he was suffering from some d.t.-induced hallucination, believing he saw something like a giant bird hovering out there above the street. The walls and the floor were shaking, a motion that brought back the sickness. A moment later, as someone swiped at the flapping curtain, he saw what it was.

A chopper.

It was a Huey, hanging there, and it was loaded with rocket pods on the skids.

Men were barking questions, confused and afraid, striking him as a bunch of unkempt school bullies.

Someone raised the panic level all around next when he announced that men with assault rifles just barged into the lobby. Wilson was about to kill another shot, get his nerves under control, when Crofton barked at him, "Lose the bottle and hit the hall."

"What's going on?" Wilson bleated.

"We've got company, mate, and I don't think these blokes came to serve tea and muffins!"

THREE STORIES UP, thirteen hardmen were in the presidential suite. No one else was allowed in the old hotel but the pack of thugs. So far the intel Bolan had been receiving was on the money.

Bolan charged through the lobby, M-16 and the rocket launcher good to go, Tolley on his heels. The old clerk came alive behind his desk. Bolan clipped him across the jaw with the assault rifle's butt, sending him to the floor. With all the racket he intended to make, Bolan didn't need the old-timer pushing any panic buttons, bringing in the cops and having the place sealed off before Bolan nailed it down. The war paint was off, but by the time the old man was able to come up with a description for the authorities, Bolan would be long gone. Flying around Port Moresby in a Huey, with two men shooting up the town, was sure to draw the eyes of every cop out and about.

It was all a gamble, but he was willing to chance it. Sure, he could have bypassed this stop altogether, focused on getting to the back door of North Korea for the main event. But the bunch of mercs and cutthroats up top were sitting on a handsome war chest for one thing. He had no need for the money personally, but the Executioner wanted to leave behind a message for any guilty parties who survived the coming blitz.

A half million in cash, seized by him, would raise eyebrows. Some of the hardmen would be left standing when the smoke cleared, and Bolan hoped absconding with the cash would leave any walking guilty in the power structure to eat each other up.

He pushed the button on the elevator and hopped out before the doors closed. It clanked to life and began rising. It was a dicey proposition all around, hoping their attention above was torn between Grimaldi blowing off the roof with rotor wash and the grind and clank of the elevator catching their attention.

The Executioner took the stairs, combat senses electrified. On the second floor he heard pounding feet, men shouting out the alarm.

He was going in blind, no fix on numbers or where the steps exited on the third floor.

He curled his finger around the M-203's trigger.

Time to bring down the roof.

WILSON WAS JUST as in the dark about what was happening as the others, but it was a damn safe bet that trouble was on the way. He saw Crofton and couple of the men stepping toward the elevator, dead center of the hall. Wilson was hugging the wall beside the wide-open double doors to the suite, taking in the fear and panic all around.

The chopper was still suspended outside the suite, he found. A few of the Aussies were flapping their hands around, sounding off the nervous questions. If they were thinking the same thing he was—the bag—this could turn into some free-for-all to grab the loot when it hit the fan.

They were being hit; that was about all Wilson could say. But by whom? Why?

The money. They were coming for the money.

The elevator was shuddering to a stop, Crofton and the others realizing they'd been duped, the cage empty, when something snared Wilson's attention. It was a zigging blur in the corner of his eye, but there was no mistaking what it was when the blast shredded Crofton and his group in smoke and fire. The rolling fireball had enough punch behind it to knock Wilson off his feet. The blistering ring of autofire was next, but Wilson found himself on his back, somewhere down the foyer. The Aussies were running past him, filling up the doorway, returning fire at their attackers, as if they could stand up to what was being thrown at them.

Rockets and grenades being blasted off in their faces, and Wilson compared their puny subguns to toothpicks in the eye of that kind of storm.

Choking down the vomit, Wilson struggled to his feet. The bag! If he could reach it in time, well, it was a three-story jump to the street. There was an overhang by the lobby and if he used that as some shaky DZ...

He was staggering away from the foyer, just in time, he realized, when the second explosion sent bodies and pieces of men flying past, something wet and heavy slapping him in the back of the head.

THE EXECUTIONER'S opening 40 mm wallop cleared them out by the elevator. He was loading another missile and breaking cover when they fell into the doorway.

He needed them routed in a hurry, so there was no sense in dragging out some bitter and extended exchange of shooting.

The second round was on the way when the bullets started snapping over his head and he was rolling down the hallway. He figured four hardmen were blown to smithereens when the rocket slammed into the doorway. How many were left?

Bolan barged into the roiling smoke, shooting from the hip, sweeping the autofire around the foyer as he sidled across the opening. Two hardmen were gagging and struggling to get back into play. They were nearly off their knees when the Executioner's spray of doom kicked them off their feet, sending them tumbling down the short flight of steps leading to the living room.

Tolley took up his position on the other side.

Before the hit, Bolan had roughly laid out how he wanted it done. He pulled a flash-stun grenade off his webbing, and Tolley took one sense-shattering egg for himself, pulling the pin, then they lobbed them through the opening in sync.

Bolan pulled back, hugged the wall, squeezed his eyes shut and covered his ears.

"WHAT THE HELL are you doing? Where are you going?"

Wilson heard the Aussie screaming at him as he headed for the bar, eyes fixed on the bag. He turned and saw the Aussie striding his way, eyes filled with rage.

"You little American fuck! You're not thinking what I think you're thinking, are you?"

He was lifting his Uzi, Wilson sure the man was

going to gun him down, then the room seemed to vanish in blinding light and a sound of thunder that pierced his eardrums like hot needles. The Aussie was gone, caught in the blast, only Wilson couldn't be certain since he seemed to go deaf and blind at the same instant. The double pounding had dropped him to his belly, rendering him a blind snake that could only manage to crawl.

He was alive, though, pain signaling him he was still in the fray. Only he was bailing, no matter what. He could feel his way to the bag, grab it up, stagger for the window and attempt the jump. The bastards had used flash-stuns, and it would take a few agonizing moments, he guessed, before he could even begin to get his senses back.

Mentally, he began crawling toward the bag, tasting the bitter bile on his lips. He only needed a few minutes, hoping the others could hold back the hitters.

BOLAN LED THE CHARGE into the suite. There were survivors, but they were in no shape to make a stand.

Still, they tried, desperate men flinging around wild autofire in hopes of saving the stash.

With Tolley beside him, Bolan worked a field of fire around the suite. They were dropping, chopped up by autofire, head to toe, the Executioner burning up a clip to mow them down. A few moaners in the corner of the room, grabbing for weapons, and Bolan was locked and loaded again. Old and tacky furniture was shredded, windows were blown out, the television on the floor— even two ceiling fans had been blown out of place, leaving a spider web of tangled wires.

Two hardmen rose near the doors to what Bolan suspected was a bedroom. Tolley joined him in waxing those two, the double punch of 5.56 mm rounds launching them back.

All done, Bolan thought as he searched the litter of bodies, glass and debris.

Not quite.

He saw the man near the bar, a human snail dragging himself along.

And trying to haul in the big nylon bag.

Bingo.

The Executioner went to the window first. The curtain had been flayed to tatters by all the shrapnel, giving Bolan a bird's-eye view of the street below. He made eye contact with Grimaldi, gave him the thumbs-up, then hand signaled for him to drop down. The street was packed with market stalls, a gaggle of locals and tourists in aloha shirts gawking now at the hotel.

Time to bolt.

Bolan marched to the bar. "I'll take that," he told the last survivor.

"You'll have to."

The man was obviously trying to focus in on the voice as a measuring stick for his Ingram. He was sweeping it around when Bolan drove a quick burst up his back.

"Let's vacate," the Executioner told Tolley, and hauled up the spoils of the hit.

11

Pappy Dooley hit the Old Bum's Tavern every morning whether he had to work that day or not. The day usually belonged to him, pissing it away, boozing it up with the other blokes. Their voices fading back to yesteryear, a bunch of grousing and grumbling about where it all went wrong maybe for each of them, but they were tough men who had known grim times and were now somehow holding on to hope that there was a future still, perhaps, even for washed-up mercs and expats without a pot to piss in.

And sometimes there was work to be done.

The Aussie expat, even on a workday, polished off a few shots of whiskey, nursing a beer or two to help him warm up for the task at hand, whatever it was. A head swimming in booze sometimes even inspired a creative angle when torturing a hapless bloke—who didn't want to pay up—that he might not have thought of stone-cold sober.

Funny how that worked.

Well, there was always some new use for a chain saw

or pliers or whatever else was available. He often dreamed up these methods after a morning's session with his mates before the call came in and the day's work was farmed out. Work usually involved collecting the provincial governor's cut from the pimps and other blokes who ran the backroom gaming parlors around Port Moresby. Sometimes the day held a few surprises if some cop turned up and wanted more than his rightful share of the take or if one the gaming boys was suspected of holding out on the governor.

It seemed to happen all too often these days. Times were tough, he figured.

And in PNG truly only the strong survived. It was a land stuffed to the gills with thieves, murderers, bastards and whores, where a few kinas were usually earned through theft, beating, extortion, corruption or outright murder. Another sip of whiskey and he thought how he always loved those *National Geographic* types who flew in on private jets, weighted down with cameras, grinning around like schoolboys, wanting to hype how PNG was the world traveler's last stop before heaven.

Thinking the rest of the world could go straight to hell, naive foreigners at the top of the list, at least he knew where he could find his other expat mates, bright and early every morning, without fail, gainfully employed that day or not. They were lined up at the bar, ten in all, strung down the bar front while Toots Barber chain-smoked and paid more attention to the American cable news station piped in, thanks to the wonders of modern satellite technology. The big story was the terrorist attacks in America. They ran the same piece every thirty minutes. How many times could Barber watch the same damn thing? he wondered. Every time the reporter mentioned the body count, though, Barber came to, straightening up, eyes alive, as if death and disaster fed some voyeuristic fantasy, as if he could peep in the window to the great society and get off over all those Americans being wasted while they went about another day in the life.

Well, routine was out the window these days for all Americans. It seemed some Iraqis had slipped into New York, Chicago and L.A., blowing up people, places and things, throwing their whole country to the edge of anarchy and revolution in the streets. Scattered riots around the States, with the National Guard and Army having descended where the firestorms erupted, trying to stem the tide of chaos with tanks, rubber bullets and fire hoses.

Screw them. It was not his problem. He had the day ahead of him to worry about. Who wouldn't pay, for one thing. Who was holding out on the governor. What constables wanted more money. Or some other less exciting chore, like driver duty. This day was one of those off days, since the work had been assigned the past night.

He already knew what to expect, and the day ahead held all the excitement of watching paint dry.

At eleven sharp he was supposed to drive to the Ela Beach Hotel, pick up the bagmen from Sydney. From there he was to take them to the old Port Moresby Hotel, where they'd collect the payday for the higher-ups in the Australian military who coddled the big shots in Port Moresby. Fat cash for everyone but himself and his merc mates. It was a game these days, he thought, killing his shot of whiskey and firing up a cigarette, who could grab up the biggest slice of grease money. A half million was on tap for the big boys, and there he was, getting soused, then driving around, watching them while they sliced up their cuts and headed back to his homeland, not a care in the world as long as the payoff money kept rolling through their fingers.

Human eels, he thought.

Slippery as the day was long.

He felt the somber mood, all around, weighing him down to his stool.

A few of the boys were back in the corner, muttering something among themselves, twitching around, antsy to get on with it. Sometimes he wasn't sure it was a good thing for all these armed men—most of whom hadn't known a decent dollar in their lives—to sit around and tie on a load, dwelling on their borderline poverty while they drove and played tour guide and bodyguard and maybe poured the brandy for all the big guys in Port Moresby and from Australia.

Life seemed to be passing him by. Pushing fifty and what the hell had he done with his life? Scrounge up chump change here and there, breaking a few heads when somebody got tight on the cut, or even worse on occasion when word of a hard lesson needed to get passed around town.

"Toots," Dooley snarled, setting his empty shot glass down with a thud. "While I'm still young and handsome, eh?"

Barber was going for the rack, scowling, of course, plucking up a bottle when Dooley heard the rusty hinges to the front door groan. He wasn't sure what he saw at first, blinking at the harsh glare of sunlight swelling the doorway before it shut and two shadows stepped inside.

"What the fuck?"

He heard himself say it, but he was still unsure of what he saw, wincing, swiping at the trickle of overflow whiskey down the side of his mouth.

Two men, one of them big and lean, scanning the crowd. Both were armed with M-16s, walking in as if they had some serious business on their minds.

No, as if they owned the joint, he decided.

The shorter one stepped off to the side, leaving his mate all alone. The big man's cold blue eyes narrowed to slits, but outshining the subdued threat of violence he felt simmering from his mates. The big man was holding a fat bag. He dumped it on a round table near the bar.

The big man in black told the crowd, "Charles Wiggins is out of business. Your mates down the street at the hotel...?"

It was a hanging question, probing, taunting, he believed. The silence and tension seemed to paralyze Dooley to his stool, but he felt his hand instinctively lowering for the .45 Colt ACP on his hip.

"Who the hell are you?" Dooley snarled.

"I'm the guy who relieved a half million from your pals just now at the hotel."

BOLAN KNEW there was a chance they wouldn't bite, perhaps try to brazen it out with lies and manipulative innocence. Going in, he put the plan together, but he and Tolley hadn't done too shabby so far, figuring it out as they went along. They were thinning out the savage herd in a hurry, catching them off guard, some half-asleep, some too hungover to make a serious threat.

So far.

This was another smash-and-bang stop, but all it would take was one well-placed or even lucky bullet and either Bolan or Tolley or both...

No time for fatalistic thinking.

Bolan knew the window was closing. And the soldier wanted in on the North Korea blitz.

Even still, there was work left to be done in PNG.

The Old Bum's Tavern by the waterfront was laid out by the CIA man in Port Moresby as a combination watering hole and business establishment for the gunmen of one Peter Towner. Bolan could have skipped this stop, since time, cops and the Huey's fuel were major considerations. But he'd come this far, cleaning up the shadow power structure that let Morton and his Doomsday Army hunker down in the jungle. And with the full weight of the American military, Justice, FBI and CIA on standby, ready to practically invade PNG, he figured he still had a few good cards left to play before he vacated Port Moresby.

And there was still the big man over in Waigani to consider for the final cleanup. Grimaldi was tied in to the CIA man's secured frequency, the spook having guided them along from stop to stop. There was always the chance, Bolan knew, it could be a dead end, with bad intel, treachery...but as the Farm's top gun soared around over the waterfront, Grimaldi was getting an update for the last call.

Towner was in, hunkered down in his office, surrounded by a goon squad. Bolan was willing to gamble Brognola's sources were playing it straight.

Right now Bolan had a full plate to consume.

The Executioner saw them tensing up, greedy eyes flickering toward the money bag, their thoughts racing through the fog of beer and whiskey, but they were seconds away from going for broke. Pride had seized the better of them. That, and they figured they had the numbers on their side.

And greed, a half million sitting there right before them, begging to be taken and divided up since their mates at the hotel had fallen on the hardest of times.

Ten down the bar, three in the far corner, with Tolley easing up to take a post behind a wide wooden beam. As waterfront bars went, it was typical from what Bolan saw. Drab, bleak decor, reeking of human misery and desperation, vomit, piss and blood spilled from past brawls. The fact every man there was armed told the soldier they'd stepped into the right—or wrong—place.

"What?" a man midway down the bar growled. He looked at his pals, chuckling, but it was saving-face noise. "You come to arrest us?"

"Not exactly," Bolan said, saw a few hands falling over the butts of pistols. He brought up the M-16, holding back on the trigger.

The Executioner mowed them down. The closest four fell off their stools when he nailed them with a burst of autofire that marched on, 5.56 mm rounds coring through two more skulls, the whole flying mess washing shocked faces with blood and brains.

They were up now, just the same, thugs bouncing off each other, guns drawn and banging out rounds.

In the far corner, the soldier glimpsed the threesome lurching to their feet, pistols up and tracking, but shock and brains sodden by liquor gave the edge to Tolley. Trapped in the booth, they were finished in three or four seconds as Tolley dropped a lead curtain over their private powwow, bodies crashing to the floor in a tangle of limbs.

The bartender became a point of grim concern for Bolan next. As Tolley fired on, tagging two runners and sending them sailing over a table, Bolan was bringing the M-16 around, seeking to gain cover at the end of the bar, when the shotgun reared up. A heartbeat slower and Bolan would have been decapitated. But his rising stitch up the bartender's torso was a little too much for the man, his body reacting to the sponging of lead, the throes of death taking over like a clamping vise. The twin barrels thundered, up and to the side. The television was obliterated in a volcanic eruption of smoke and sparks.

Four left, and they were jerking around in the middle of the room, taking hits from Tolley, but cursing out their rage and trying to line up their pistols.

The Executioner fired on, nearly scalped by a scorching round or two, but he sidled out into the open, raking the M-16 back and forth, catching them torn between two shooters. The double scissoring of auto-fire wrapped it up in a few more heartbeats, as dancing hardmen, dead on their feet, flopped over tables or plunged to the greasy floor, splashing gore where they fell.

Bolan checked on Tolley and tuned in for any sounds of movement from the bathroom down the hall.

No more takers. Just in case, he'd watch his back on the way out.

The DIA man was nodding around at the carnage. There was a new look in Tolley's eyes, Bolan saw, a blood lust seeming to get more fevered with each killing pit stop. Was he grinning? Was he losing it to a sense of tarnished pride and months on the run? Looking to regain some former stature?

"You ever get used to this, Belasko?"

"Used to what?"

"All the killing?"

"Never. Just like I never get used to what I see in men like these."

"Yeah, well, I can see how exterminating the rats can give a man a reason to live."

Bolan wasn't quite sure how to respond to that.

"Why are you looking at me like that?" Tolley asked. "Like I'm some alien just came down through the ceiling."

"This is a job, Tolley, not an adventure."

"Saying you want me to bow out?"

"Pull it together. This is no day at the beach. Let's roll."

The Executioner considered dropping a thermite grenade into the money bag, then decided the spoils of war could get turned over to Brognola and put to better use to work for the good guys. Similar, he supposed, to DEA seizures of drug money and assets.

Why not?

The bad guys had been living high, mighty and free too long in PNG. A half million wasn't much in terms of what had been dumped into Morton's operation, but lost money was just that.

Somebody would feel the sting.

And there was one more somebody to bite, Bolan thought, before Port Moresby became a bad memory in a campaign already littered with nightmares.

PETER TOWNER STARED out the window of his top-floor office suite, wondering what in the world was happening around Port Moresby. The Waigani constable, Tucker, was on the speakerphone, his breath coming out in long gasps as he related an incredible story of horror and carnage.

Towner turned away from the sight of the first set of players trundling out in carts across the green-carpeted expanse of the golf course. What Tucker relayed to him was beyond unbelievable. By God, it was a disaster, a nightmare, even doomsday rolled into one, and Towner had to wonder if he was next to get blown down by the human storm raging across town.

If more money was the answer, he'd gladly dole out whopping sums to have the madmen hunted down and shot where they stood. He had all the money in the world, old-world money, having climbed to the top pretty much the way the late Charles Wiggins had come by his fortune.

Heritage.

Gold, silver and copper, men with guns and bad attitudes who went out and made things happen over the years for him when the politicians became nervous old hens.

That now seemed like a million light-years away.

What was happening all over Port Moresby had clearly rattled Tucker, and Towner was considering a long vacation, maybe Tokyo, until things calmed down. He'd leave the dirty work to the men whose bank accounts he fattened on a monthly basis. Better yet, he'd wait until hard justice was returned in kind to the madmen and it was absolutely safe for him to come back to Port Moresby.

"Slow down, Constable," Towner said. "Get control of yourself. You have a sizable police force under you that you can marshal and send out to hunt these *three* men down. We have, I believe, four helicopters that can go up and intercept this Huey that is transporting these two lunatics all over town."

"You don't understand."

"So, clue me in."

"What pilots I have available are...unavailable."

"How's that?"

"They disappear at the most inopportune times. Whores and hangovers keep them calling in sick all the time, if they call in at all."

"Most irresponsible. I suggest we take a hard look at that situation. You're telling me this Huey came from up the Fly River?"

"Yes."

"Morton? Turning against us?"

Tucker groaned. "No. Why stab us in the back?"

"Money. Perhaps they are tired of paying us."

"I don't believe so."

Towner plopped down in the wing chair behind his desk. He stared at the massive oak doors leading out to the receptionist bay. The entire workforce in the building had been given the day off, no secretary out there, Miss Tyler dismissed from duty when he'd first received word an hour or so ago about the madmen blowing through Port Moresby. Instead, he'd brought in four of the best Aussie ex-military men money could buy to make sure he didn't become another casualty. He wondered if four men would be enough, considering the body count that was multiplying with each call from Tucker. Wiggins, his politicians and bankers and their entire security force had been wiped out at his beachfront estate. Then the bagmen at the hotel, his best mercs, shot down and blown up in their suite, the money destined to pay off his Australian counterparts taken by the mystery hit men. Now a report that Pappy Dooley and his gang had been massacred where they sat, whiling away the morning in booze and telling dirty jokes—the usual—with witnesses on the street describing two men with M-16s, both of whom were snapped up by this Huey as they left the tavern. Well, if someone had been watching all three locales, none of the massacred were hard to find, with the hunters able to establish some routine that would leave all those men vulnerable to attack. Wiggins and his group had been the first to get wiped out, and it looked as if the nameless hunters had gone for the big game first—which made him think he was safe for the time being. Well, the other movers and shakers of Port Moresby had been out there for several days, fairly hiding, whining and reconsidering, from what he gathered, about the American situation up the Fly River. CIA then? Towner wondered. Not their style—they were little more than government stooges with guns and high-tech surveillance equipment. There were a few Company operatives scattered about Port Moresby, sure, monitoring the whole spectrum of what could accurately be described as Peter Towner's underworld. But this was execution, straightforward butchery, of the entire security force that belonged to him and the late Wiggins.

This smacked of payback. It all had something to do with the Americans upriver, which made him wonder about their real purpose in PNG, and if they had anything to do with the terrorist attacks in America.

"What should I do?"

Towner chuckled.

"You find this amusing?"

"Find these men, Constable, and deal with them. You are paid very well to make sure unpleasant situations are handled."

"Just like that?"

"Call me when you have results."

The constable started squawking, but Towner curtly cut him off, telling him that was all before punching off the speakerphone.

Towner made his decision. It was time to bail, ride out the storm somewhere else. He picked up the phone to call in his chopper.

A sound jerked him up out of his chair.

He'd heard his own chopper land on the roof enough times to know the slight trembling beneath his feet for what it was—rotor wash. A helicopter had landed, and he wanted to assume his own pilot was a mind reader, but a cold nagging fear warned him he wasn't.

He was punching on the intercom, barking for one of his security detail to go up top when the muted stutter of weapons fire sounded beyond his doors.

The nameless killers had arrived. He couldn't help but wonder if they had saved him for last, and wanted to chuckle over his own sense of self-importance.

As if he'd been at the top of the list all along.

No way would he sit there and get gunned down in his own office, a trapped rat like the others. He flung open the top drawer and armed himself with the .45-caliber pistol.

Maybe Wiggins and the others went down without a fight, caught napping or too hungover, but some primal fear and hatred of the moment told Towner it was better to stand tall and take it on the chin than bow and ask for mercy. He would see what happened in the coming moments, either way.

There was money to think about, an empire to salvage. He could get his hands on far more than the paltry half million the mercs at the hotel had been murderously relieved of, and he was willing to give up a little to try to save his world.

A slim chance, bargaining with these devils, but he'd try to buy his way out.

HE WAS A NEW MAN, reborn, the phoenix rising from the ashes. He had run for too damn long but now he'd been given some new lease on life.

Tolley was fighting back, standing tall against the demons in human skin who had haunted his every waking and sleeping moment for months.

All the fear he'd sucked on before now, while heaping his thoughts with all the remembrance of a life pretty much swamped in failure. Marriage gone to hell. Kids who didn't want to know he existed. Maneuvering himself smack in the middle of the greatest conspiracy— probably in history—and at one point in the beginning even straddling the fence, wondering if he should take the money...

No way. He didn't have much, but he had his soul, and that was not for sale.

The former life was all but forgotten now that he had a reason to live, even if that meant dying in the heat of combat. Yesterday, he thought, was nothing more than a dirty shirt he'd shed to put on the glistening armor of a warrior.

Not only that, but with each shot he fired in anger, with each body he saw topple under his M-16, Tolley felt a jolt of excitement he didn't think he could have ever imagined.

It was that time again.

Show time.

Maybe it was Belasko or the flyboy displaying all the nerve required to mop up the bad guys, that was fueling him with inspiration to move into the next killing field. Whatever. He wasn't going to let anybody down at this point, least of all himself. Before the blacksuits had showed up to wax his butt that anxious night, he could have never imagined himself wading into full-scale battle, hanging it out there, toe-to-toe, gun blazing, feeling himself wanting to laugh at the very notion of his own sudden death.

But there he was. And as far as he was concerned, he had as much right to be there as Belasko. He had the same heart and hunger.

And the killing seemed like an intoxicant, the best elixir under God's sun.

Better than booze.

He couldn't be sure what it was really, but he was hopped up on the adrenaline, the fire in his blood turning hotter with every kill to wax some more dirty bastards.

They were coming down the service stairwell, Belasko having laid out the hit before the Huey settled on the rooftop helipad, Tolley taking point as instructed. He heard them already scuffling and barking questions around the corner, getting it together or trying to make a stand. Bad news among bad guys, he knew, traveled fast, so he reckoned they were expected.

Not a problem.

Tolley crouched at the foot of the steps. A look around the corner and he took in the receptionist area. Four of them, flying around with compact subguns, looking silly somehow in their fear and confusion.

Tolley tagged one of them out of the gate, a short burst that ripped open the silk-shirted goon across the chest as he charged around the corner of the horseshoe-shaped reception bay. Once again, the two of them had no idea on the numbers, although the Company man had spelled it out, but who the hell could he really trust at this stage to get it right and get it done?

Except Belasko.

The big man lobbed a grenade in the direction of the three hardmen sweeping around the opposite edge of the horseshoe.

Bingo.

When it blew, chunks of the goon squad were plastered in red greasy smears across the polished teak walls and picture frames, while palm trees came apart, glass and foliage winging all over the place.

And Tolley moved out, on fire from head to toe, hoping to hell somebody came running down the hall.

No one did.

That left Mr. Towner, primed and waiting behind the fat double doors. He hoped that guy either begged for his life or tried to get cute and pulled a piece.

He couldn't wait to lay eyes on another big shot crying to save his world.

Tolley heard his chuckle roll from his lips as he raised his assault rifle and squeezed the M-203's trigger.

BOLAN WASN'T SURE what had come over Tolley, but he didn't have the time to consider the man's state of mind. He was bolting around the corner of the stairwell, searching for fresh targets beyond the wall of hanging smoke and heading for the double doors past Tolley. He was certain Towner was waiting beyond in his office when he heard the chug from over his shoulder.

The Executioner flinched, knew what was coming and flung his arms up in front of his face. The shock wave nearly knocked him off his feet. Less than thirty paces, and the 40 mm blast vaporized the door, puking open a smoking maw, paving the way. That wasn't Tolley's call to make, Bolan angrily thought. The guy was acting on his own now, leaving the soldier to ponder the man's psyche.

Bolan gritted his teeth, senses choked with smoke, debris slashing the air above his head or pelting his arms. "Stay here and cover my back!"

"No problem, Captain. It's your show."

The Executioner hunched, sliding off to take up position beside the obliterated opening, expecting a response.

"Towner!"

"I'm armed! I want to deal!"

Bolan pegged the voice, somewhere at twelve o'clock. The smoke was thinning beyond the jagged shards when he made out the figure, rising above a desk, a pistol extended.

"Let me walk, I can give you names, if you want. You want money, name your price."

The Executioner took up slack on the M-16's trigger. Time was up in PNG. This was the last stop. Towner knew he was a dead man, common sense telling him he was finished as some overlord of the corrupted legal and political infrastructure in PNG, and the panic rising in his voice with each word warned Bolan he was blowing smoke with his pleas for a deal. The pistol cannoned, clearly marking Towner's position for Bolan to nail it down.

The Executioner swung the M-16, low around the corner. Towner was screaming he was willing to bargain if they would just listen to reason when Bolan cut loose with a long barrage of autofire. A half-dozen rounds from the soldier's assault rifle, drilling the burst up the man's torso, and Towner dropped out of sight.

The soldier lingered for several moments, listening through the ring of autofire for any movement inside the office. Certain they were done with Towner he rose, turning toward Tolley.

"Another one bites the dust, huh, Captain?"

"Let's go," Bolan told the DIA man. "You and I need to have a little talk."

"What's the problem? You sound upset."

12

They made it.

North Korea.

Don't ask him how they did it, getting there in one piece, nor was John Wallace sure what he had expected to find at the end of the sub ride, but a part of him was glad he was there now.

Damn glad.

Small comfort, but he wasn't stuffed into a steel can anymore. He was able now to stretch his legs, get his bearings and breathe the fresh air.

It was a massive bunker, carved into what he suspected was a rocky cliff overlooking the Haeju harbor or wherever the hell they were. They were walking down the ramp thrown over the sub's deck, the American abductees practically force marched by the North Koreans toting AK-47s. They didn't look good. Clearly stressed and exhausted, the men unshaved and angry, scowling, while the women with eyes darting all around, near hysterical, were ready to snap unless he missed his guess.

Looking around he saw soldiers, cranes, crates, concrete wharves, forklifts and catwalks. It was night; that was about all he knew. He had no watch so he'd been unable to tell time unless he had wanted to sit in his bunk and count off the minutes in his head. Two, three days tops, he reckoned, crammed in his quarters with Pender, Bide and Thompkins, all of them restless and worried. But where could he go? The food had consisted of rice and some sort of oily fish soup, and his stomach was constantly growling but food was the least of his concerns. He had slept, at least, long and deep, and time had blessedly passed in slumber.

Now what? Beyond the cavernous mouth of the bunker it was black as coal out in the harbor. He was a prisoner, no mistake, and his mood matched the black seas and the black wall of rock curving above them.

He needed a gun. He had no idea what he was going to do, but he would do something.

Break out and run like hell.

This gig was dead, had been since the whole scheme had been changed by Chongjin in the middle of the game. The charter members of the Phoenix Council, stepping onto the dock while Chongjin barked orders at his soldiers, showed the strain, too. They didn't look despairing, not yet, and Wallace believed he read the same fire in their eyes.

They wanted out. And they'd do whatever was necessary, even if it cost them their lives.

"Move, people!" Chongjin yelled as the last of the

abductees staggered onto the dock. "Your quarters are this way!" he said, soldiers falling in, shoving the Americans down the dock.

Wallace, of course, knew he couldn't say what would happen next. But he knew one thing for sure.

After the Iraqis had been cut loose on American cities, murdering citizens, when the prototype Globe-Specter had been trashed and sunk to the bottom of the Pacific Ocean, turning Americans into shark chum, the might of the American military was going to descend on this place like the wrath of Hell.

"Is there a problem, Mr. Wallace?"

Chongjin was staring at him, edged out for some reason. Wallace moved off the ramp, looked at the colonel and shook his head. "No problem."

The colonel grinned. "I hope not. The best is yet to come. This is, how would you say—" he gestured around the bunker "—home sweet home?"

"Yeah. You got it. Home sweet home. It doesn't get any better than this."

IF THE STEEL WALLS, rows of metal bunks, the camera on the wall, rice and fish were the North Korean's idea of creature comforts, then Thomas Shaw knew they were in for a long stretch of more misery and hardship.

"We're finished," Dwight Parker said as the North Korean soldier slammed the steel door to their quarters.

"No one's coming to get us," Jason Monroe added. "We're stuck, trapped, forgotten."

And Shaw, fearing the moment all along, heard his

daughter shriek, erupting past her own breaking point. He grabbed her by the shoulders as she thrashed around, wailing. He had never laid a hand on his children, but he felt the strain, the terror of all the days, the memory of all the killing since they'd been abducted. It seized him, taking over, his own emotions overwhelming him. He slapped her in the face, growling her name over and over. Finally she calmed down, her body going limp as she dropped onto the bunk.

"I'm sorry...I'm sorry, Dad...."

Shaw watched his wife take his daughter in her arms. He stood there, seeing nothing, listening to the voices of despair. How they were abandoned to their fate. How no one would come and get them.

He looked at the other members of the Titan Four, now Titan Three after Blankenship was killed. "Don't talk like that, please," Shaw said.

"What?" Monroe said. "You think our people will actually invade North Korea and rescue us?"

"There's a chance. We have to stay strong. We have to hold on to hope."

Parker shook his head, wilting onto his bunk. "I wish I shared your confidence that we still have hope."

"We're little more than inmates," Monroe said.

"He's right," Janet Miles said.

Shaw looked at Miles as she sat on her bunk. "There's no way our own government will let us sit here and rot. Someone will come. When they do, I suggest we're ready."

"Ready to what?" Monroe asked.

"Fight our way out," she said.

Shaw slumped on his bunk and took his daughter in his arms. He only hoped the lady was right.

That all of them, the survivors of this nightmare, would go home.

"THERE'S GOING to be trouble."

Commander Ohm didn't want to hear about trouble. But the three intelligence operatives from Pyongyang, nameless men in dark suit jackets and buzz cuts, were warning him to pretty much cover his own ass and be prepared to bail. Particulars were sketchy, and he knew better than to ask a slew of questions of these men. They would only tell him what they wanted to anyway, leave him to his fears and his imaginings of the worst.

Apparently Kim Jong Il had decided Colonel Chongjin had become an albatross around his neck. It was a foolish venture from the beginning as far as he was concerned, but Chongjin was ambitious, bringing him on board, using the nuclear submarine, the only one his country had, using him to help stick the thumbs of North Korea into the eyes of the Americans.

Now this.

Trouble on the way.

"Could you be more specific?"

They were standing in the office above the dock. Chongjin had gone, presumably, to get the Americans situated in their quarters.

Ohm listened carefully. He was told the compound would be attacked, when and how exactly the operatives weren't sure. It seemed their illustrious leader had worked out some sort of deal with the American President.

The shortest operative did all the talking while the others watched Ohm. "There will be changes soon. There will be no coup as the colonel planned. The Iraqis were sent back to Baghdad. It is time for us to cut our losses and try to save some face."

"You are positive about this strike?" Ohm asked, wondering how much time he had to put some distance between himself and Chongjin.

"The Americans," the operative said, "are like a sleeping lion. Once roused... Their citizens were murdered and their SDI scientists abducted under their very noses."

"They must do something," Ohm said, nodding. "And the colonel?"

"He is finished. Whether it is the American strike force who takes care of him or someone else."

"And me?"

"I suggest you remain loyal to Pyongyang."

And Ohm watched them leave, filing out through the office door. The whole plan had been insane from the beginning, but Chongjin had the clout and connections. He had been something like a favored son to Kim Jong. Who could really say what went on in Kim Jong Il's head?

Ohm went to the chair behind his desk and sat. So what was he supposed to do now? Sit around and wait for the Americans to attack? Become a casualty when the bombs started falling?

Soon, he decided, he would make his way to the compound, find a vehicle and simply drive away. Pyongyang was making Chongjin a sacrificial lamb and Ohm didn't want to be anywhere near the man when his number was yanked.

THE RUNWAY at Dujan was lined up with thirty fighter jets. The Spectre was at the very end of the runway, Grimaldi at the helm.

All systems looked good to go, but Bolan wasn't so sure.

The soldier took a moment, standing on the helipad as his blacksuits loaded into the Sea Stallion. Tolley was at his side, nodding what Bolan suspected was either approval or eagerness to get on with it.

It was going to be a seventy-klick ride to the compound at Haeju by chopper. A team of Delta Force commandos, fifteen in all, was responsible for taking control of the airfield, while three of them took up sniping positions on the hills south of the installation. It was Grimaldi's job to land and pick up Bolan and the fifteen Americans being held hostage once the soldier and his team went in and rooted them out. Satellite imagery had detailed the sprawling compound and picked up the Americans as they had been marched into their quarters. It wasn't clear whether or not Kim Jong Il had given his blessing to take Chongjin out.

Well, it was striking a deal with the devil, but when the smoke finally cleared, Chongjin and his renegade army would be history and the compound leveled.

It was assuming a lot, but Bolan hadn't come this far to not get his pound of flesh from the murderous North Korean colonel.

It was eye for an eye from there on.

"You're going to need me, Belasko," Tolley said, nearly forced to shout above the rotor wash, the collective rumble of the Spectre's engines and the whine of the turbo fans on the runway. "Once we hit the States again..."

"Just remember what we talked about."

"I'm under control, don't worry about me."

"We'll worry about that cleanup list for the States if and when we take care of Haeju."

"Gotcha."

WALLACE WAS chain-smoking and pacing around the rows of bunks. The Phoenix Council was grumbling and he was sure Chongjin was listening.

"I say we make a stand," Jeffrey Hill told the group. "We force the issue, tell Chongjin to ship us back to the States."

"And do what?" the FEMA man posed. "We're traitors."

"We have men back home who can take care of us," Hill said.

"They'll deny their role."

"But they're still involved. I'm sure they're holed up somewhere right now, waiting to hear from us" Hill said. "We have to get out of here. I'm not going to be some prisoner the rest of my life in this godforsaken country."

The door opened suddenly.

The colonel, Wallace saw, stepping inside, running a dark look over their faces. And he was holding an AK-47.

"I have been listening to everything you have said," Chongjin announced.

Wallace steeled himself, ready to lunge at the man, snatch the weapon away and go for broke.

"What the hell, Colonel?" Hill said, rising from his bunk. "You going to shoot us all? Then what?"

"Perhaps I don't need you anymore. Perhaps you are too much trouble, more mouths to feed."

"Why, you..."

Chongjin took a step forward.

Wallace dropped his cigarette and felt the tension coiling inside Pender, Bide and Thompkins as his men came off their bunks.

13

It was straight payback for the most part. Beyond making certain the hostages were extracted, all fifteen alive and accounted for, it was the job of the black-ops team to hammer the North Korean installation to smoking rubble, make them taste the bitter sting of this strike for a long time to come.

Put them in their place pretty much, wax every last one of the murderous bastards—Chongjin, Phoenix Council, North Korean soldiers—and Bolan had no problem with his orders. In fact, nothing was to be left standing but rubble and strewed NK soldiers, and that included the nuclear reprocessing plant.

The cooling tower marked the heart and soul of their missile program here, rising from the plateau to the distant north. Grimaldi's job would be to take it out last, and Bolan had decided a landing on the runway for pickup might not happen after all. Instead, he would call back the Sea Stallions for the extraction.

The scorched-earth policy came from Brognola, and the green light was signaled by the Man himself to turn it all into a wasteland, radioactive or otherwise. American citizens had been murdered on their own soil, and if Tolley was right, another army of conspirators had a pipeline of men and matériel that stretched from coast to coast back at the States.

Later.

The Executioner knew he had his hands full where things stood.

No mercy, no apologies.

No way out for Chongjin.

Time to get busy. He hit the edge of the hill, M-16 in hand, leading the charge for the open ground beyond the watchtower at the southwest quadrant. The Sea Stallion lifted off, the other chopper disgorging the Delta Force commandos on the ridge to the east.

The whole complex was roughly four city blocks, but compounds always looked much larger and sprawling in person than they did on satellite imagery. This one was no exception. Building A was the responsibility of Bolan and his Alpha team to penetrate, take down and mop up whatever resistance inside. To the east, the sizeable motor pool of vans, APCs, Humvees and a smattering of luxury vehicles was left for the flying death squads. Likewise the troops barracks to the east belonged to the pilots. Of course, the Executioner anticipated encountering all manner of hostile resistance when they blew down the door and went hunting.

So be it. It was frag 'em and blast 'em where they showed.

Eight blacksuits, nine including Tolley, and Bolan gave the first wave of fighter jets time to get it started. The watchtowers around the compound were aiming the revolving halogen lights at the dark sky, white fingers scissoring the sky toward the harbor as the shrieking of turbo fans from five thousand feet up grew and closed, a sound of rushing doom. Soldiers squawked on radios in their towers, sounding the alarm, but their mouths didn't move long. Big Remington Model 700 sniper rifles began booming in unison along the ridge. Four towers, and the Delta commandos did the job, blasting out glass. The dark clouds of exploding brain matter and blood sealed their fate as they were pitched out of sight.

Building A was a short run past squat concrete bunkers. There was another motor pool spread near the gate, but Bolan had laid out what he wanted done by his team.

The motor pool would get primed to blow, in case any enemy runners thought they could beat a fast exit.

Bolan was charging for the door, two of his black-suits falling back to begin priming the motor pool with plastique, wondering how much he'd need to blow down the double lead doors, when the fighter jets began letting loose their weapons. By now, Bolan glimpsed, North Korean soldiers with AKs were barreling outside, shouting and pointing at the sky.

The formation of F-15s got the pounding started. A rolling wave of fire took out more than half the barracks, bodies twirling away from the conflagration as if they were belched from the eye of a hurricane.

The Executioner was about to break past the motor pool and sprint for the door when shadows popped up along Building A's edge and began unleashing a storm of autofire.

THE THUNDER PEALED, long, loud and hard. The walls of the quarters trembled, the roof sounding as if it would drop on their heads, and no one needed to read each other's expressions to know what was happening.

It was over, and Wallace knew the full wrath of the American military was razing the compound.

End game.

Chongjin lowered the assault rifle, a dark scowl on his face.

"Now what?" Hill demanded.

"That's a black-ops team. There will be shock troops inside this building any second to take back those hostages," Henry Jacklin cried.

"And they won't be coming in to offer us a sweetheart deal if we hand back the hostages and go back to America," the FEMA man growled.

Wallace watched as Chongjin smiled at him and his men, said, "You four I need." Then he told the Phoenix Council, "You four I don't."

He was raising the AK-47, the members cursing, pleading for their lives.

Hill was springing forward, mind snapping from rage over this treachery, when Chongjin turned on the killing sweep. He hit them point-blank, raking the flaming line of bullets back and forth, chopping them up where they stood. Hill held on, cursing like a madman, even as he danced back, the other three already toppling.

Chongjin planted a burst in Hill's face and ended the matter.

"Okay, Colonel," Wallace said, practically shouting from the ringing in his ears due to the close proximity to the autofire, the floor still shaking beneath his feet as the fighters outside bombed on, a sound of Armageddon. "We need weapons if you want our help."

"Yes. This way. Then we get the hostages. If you try something funny..."

"I've got the picture. Say no more."

Wallace gave his men an uncertain look, his heart hammering from fear, aware this was quite possibly the end.

All the time, trouble and risk to get it to this point, and now the whole damn dream of the Phoenix Council was about to go down the toilet.

It didn't make sense. It didn't seem right to Wallace, but he'd help Chongjin up to a point, then find a way to bail. In all the chaos and confusion of battle there would be a way to run.

There had to be.

ALPHA TEAM WAS DRIVEN to cover at the far edge of the motor pool. Bullets slashed asphalt near his feet, spanged off metal near Bolan's head. Thanks to the sea of fire that was eating up the parked MiGs, helicopter gunships and other aircraft from the airfield, the Executioner grabbed a head count of the rooftop hardforce.

Ten, some kneeling, some standing, some stretched out in prone positions. The problem was time, running out by the second, since he was sure Chongjin would grab the hostages and go for some back-door exit.

Bolan keyed his com-link, already judging the toss. Twenty feet up, thirty down.

"All of you, grab a grenade. I need that roof cleared two minutes ago. Let's do it."

Bolan pulled the pin on his frag grenade. The blacksuits realized the urgency of getting to that door, so not a second more was wasted, as they lurched up and hurled the bombs. The steel eggs dropped among the shooters, a line of bouncing sudden death that covered the entire gallery of hardmen. Ten blasts, most of them going off as one, with the others delaying their knockout punch by a heartbeat or two, and the whole blazing picture shredded the NK soldiers, men screaming and flying out from the fireballs, crunching to the asphalt.

Clear.

A check of the troop barracks, and Bolan was just in time to watch the second wave of Sparrows and Sidewinders, which had been recalibrated for air to ground. The Executioner couldn't believe anything could possibly walk, crawl or limp from that holocaust.

The Executioner gave the order for two blacksuits to take the far west edge of the building, make their way to the back and seal it off.

Bolan made the door and gave the word for his blast man to prime it up with enough C-4 to blow the damn thing off its hinges.

He nodded and went to work while the F-15s dropped in next to hammer whatever was left standing on the airfield, the bulk of missile concentration lighting up the SAM antiaircraft batteries.

"Sir, I suggest we haul it back to the motor pool."

Bolan checked the load of plastique fixed to the center line of the door, spread up and down the edges of the jamb, all of it wired up for one electronic touch. If this didn't do the trick and get them in, he'd have to direct one of the fighters to blow the damn thing off the building.

The Executioner raced back for the motor pool, his senses choked with blood, emptied bowels and bladders, the gritty stink of burning rocket fuel wafting his way from the distant inferno.

From there on, even once they got inside, easy would be left to the dead.

THE TERRIBLE THUNDER outside the building had Shaw and the others leaping out of their bunks. For the first time since being abducted, he actually thought he saw hope in their eyes. He knew he at least felt hope in his heart, but now what?

Someone was bombing up the entire facility, and no one there needed to say who that was.

Rescue.

"They came to get us!" Monroe said, looking giddy but sounding afraid.

"We're not free yet," Shaw said.

"Nor are you going to be."

Chongjin marched into their quarters. He was surrounded by his soldiers. The four Americans were also armed with AK-47s.

"You will come with us. You will do what you are told, when you are told," Chongjin shouted. "Any resistance, any hesitation, I will simply start shooting. Move!"

Apparently they didn't move fast enough, as Shaw found the soldiers grabbing them and shoving them ahead. Outside in the wide hallway, Shaw, sticking close to his wife and daughter, started marching, ringed in by the colonel and his soldiers, the four Americans leading the way. He wanted to tell his family to remain calm. There was a chance they would be gone from there soon.

But gone, he thought, how? And in what shape? Gone as in going home?

Or gone as in dead?

If guns were turned on them, Shaw determined he would make some desperate lunge and try to wrestle one of the weapons away. He wouldn't stand by and watch his family and the others murdered in cold blood.

Not after everything they endured.

Not when there was hope.

He saw more soldiers rolling around the corner, Chongjin barking orders, when another massive explosion sounded from somewhere in the building behind them.

"Faster! Faster!" Chongjin shouted at the pack, as Shaw watched the platoon of soldiers charge past.

THE EXECUTIONER was the first one into the smoke. He was clearing the cloud, M-16 up and tracking. They were in some long, wide corridor with concrete walls when the first group of armed resistance showed up.

Alpha team wasted no time. Three chugs merged as one sound, the trio of 40 mm grenades zigging on. The North Korean soldiers began pounding out the autofire, then froze at the sight of doomsday racing their way. Some turned, hollering in their own tongue and tried to run, but it was too late for them. The explosions scattered them in every direction, pinning bodies to the walls, two figures rising for the ceiling before plunging back into the wall of smoke.

Two blacksuits watched their rear, as Bolan and Tolley advanced. They came to a massive room that housed rows of computers and wall maps of the world. Giant computer screens were glowing with what he suspected were the specs for ballistic missiles.

Another platoon of North Korean soldiers came running into the workroom from a door on the opposite side. Again Bolan didn't want to get bogged down trading fire while Chongjin tried to pull a vanishing act.

Still, he couldn't leave enemy shooters on his heels. The Executioner loaded up another 40 mm hellbomb in the M-203. Tolley peeled off to his left as the autofire cut loose from across the room, the blacksuits sticking with Bolan as they crouched and sidled down behind a row of computers.

Three 40 mm missiles were sailing on, and the blasts obliterated a whole area of machines and maps. Somewhere in the smoke, Bolan heard groaning and choking. Four mangled bodies had been dumped on large worktables, but the soldier knew he had a few walking wounded to deal with.

In a room like this, a maze of work bays, partitions and glass cubicles, anything could happen.

It did.

He saw the grenade coming out of the smoke, flying right his way. The soldier, scrambling for cover behind a partition, yelled, "Hit the deck!"

14

Autofire and grenade blasts echoed down the next maze of halls, interspersed with men shouting out the pain and horror of their final seconds. No question, this place was going down. Wallace knew they were all in a world of hurt, North Korean or American. His mind was fevered by fear, wondering how many black-ops invaders were right then swelling up the place, on the hunt, ready to nail all their butts, no questions asked.

Chongjin's own soldiers kept showing up, on the run, getting their orders to go fight. And probably die. Where did he get all these soldiers? No matter, he thought, as long as their evac was covered, Wallace didn't give a damn how many men Chongjin lost. He was sending them to certain death. This show was over, and all Wallace wanted was a quick exit stage left.

How and when? And after he pulled the plug on Chongjin, then what?

"This way!" Chongjin shouted.

The whole herd was shoved down another corridor by the colonel's soldiers. At the end of the corridor an offshoot hall led to the gate that was open to some massive warehouse. It was stuffed with crates, forklifts, cranes and other machinery he couldn't identify. Chongjin was busy shouting at the hostages to move faster, so Wallace decided he wouldn't get a better chance, especially with all the rolling thunder of grenades going off and swelling the air around them.

Wallace whispered to Pender, "Be ready when I make my move."

Pender nodded. They knew what to do.

Chongjin would be dead meat as soon as they hit that warehouse.

IT WAS CLOSE. Still, Bolan would have been diced had he not flung himself behind the partition as he heard the grenade thunking under some desk dead ahead. He caught sight of the other blacksuits and Tolley flying over desks themselves, taking his warning to heart, grabbing shelter from the storm wherever they could find it.

Nothing to do now but hold on and hope, ride it out, keep going, hunting, hitting hard and fast.

The grenade blew, the top half of the partition getting smashed in the blast, hurling plaster over Bolan's head, filling his nose with smoke.

There was no time to waste or allow the enemy to get another grenade primed and thrown. The Executioner whipped around the corner, crouched and heard the bursts of autofire nearby, telling him his guys were still in play, joining him in the return barrage.

Bolan saw them, four shooters bobbing and weaving

through the maze of partitions and work bays, firing on the run. He let them have it with a well-placed 40 mm round. They were kicked back from the fireball, going down hard and skidding along, the blast bringing down the partition, shredded by shrapnel.

"Cover me," Bolan told his teammates, rolling out, his senses tuned in on the groaners.

He made the corner of a workstation, cautiously peeking into the open.

There were two of them, bloody human rags, struggling to find their assault rifles in the scattered trash of computers and other debris. One looked Bolan's way, shouting something, then the Executioner finished them off with two quick bursts.

An explosion from somewhere behind Bolan jolted him to new danger. He was wheeling around when he discovered one of his blacksuits had all but obliterated the glass wall that ran down the side of the work area. Beyond the smoke of the 40 mm blast, North Korean soldiers were hopping around, rubbing their eyes, probably nailed by flying glass and shrapnel. Marching back to join his teammates, the Executioner held back on the M-16's trigger, helping them punch holes through the smoke cloud with extended salvos of autofire.

All done for the moment, more NK soldiers toppling from sight or cut to ribbons. Bolan led the race back out into the hallway, feeding his M-16 a fresh clip, the M-203 filled with a hellbomb, ready to keep working hard to clear rooms and take down the enemy.

He came to a corridor and heard a voice shouting in English.

"Move it! Move it!"

Chongjin.

Luck, fate or cosmic justice pulling him along, it didn't matter. Bolan had the smell of blood in his nose. Each step, each kill, only meant he had to ratchet it all up a notch.

The Executioner homed in on the angry voice.

COMMANDER OHM WAS stunned by the vast and utter destruction he found waiting as he jogged toward the vehicles that were somehow left unscathed by the bombardment. Strange, he thought, all vehicles near the ruins of the soldier barracks were flaming scrap. Why only wipe out that motor pool?

Well, he saw an opening now, just the same, figuring some oversight on behalf of the attackers. In the heat of combat, mistakes were made. That was the only thing he could think of to account for leaving him a ride out of there. The American commandos had just blown the door and gone in when he crept out of the bunk that led to the dock belowground. Pistol in hand, he tried to search for armed shadows, but couldn't find any gunmen right away. Then he heard the blistering of weapons fire near the airfield.

Or, rather, what was left of it.

Incredible. The soldiers's barracks had been reduced to flaming rubble. More than one hundred North Koreans, all of them special forces, blown to smithereens where they either slept in the dead of night or came to in a lurch and cry of alarms, alerted by the shriek of the incoming American fighter jets.

And the skies were swarming with winged killers, zipping all around, searching for something to blow up. What was left? There was the submarine bunker cut into the side of the harbor's cliff, but it wouldn't take much effort for a few F-15s to come in low across the harbor and bring the cavern dock down. There was also the nuclear-waste reprocessing plant with several ICBMs stored there.

The Americans, he feared, were saving the biggest and the best for last.

It seemed like no better time than the present to bail.

He made the van and found the keys inside.

Beautiful.

From there he'd ride to Pyongyang and try to throw himself back into the good graces of Kim Jong Il. There were many plausible explanations he could hand the man, short of groveling for mercy. Chongjin was insane, but by the time he figured it out, it was too late. Flattery might score some points with Kim Jong, too, stroke the man's ego, tell him he was the savior of North Korea with his wisdom and foresight in seeing how treacherous and crazy the colonel was. Surely the great leader could see the commander had been duped and was ready to make amends and come back into the fold, make it all right somehow.

He was keying the ignition, ready to tromp the gas when a black-garbed figure stepped from out of the shadows of the bunker, framed in his rearview mirror, and holding something in his hand.

It kicked in next what the something was, and Commander Ohm bellowed in frustration and terror before the world blew up in his eyes, the fireball tearing through him, lifting him out of his seat and through the roof, incinerated.

WALLACE SAW THEM, five blacksuits with M-16s charge through the warehouse gate. They spread out, sliding off in different directions, using machinery and crates as cover. Their com-links were in place to stay in touch at a moment's notice.

Pros.

They were going for some outflanking move to seal them in and end it.

"Colonel, you've got a problem on your back side," Wallace said.

Chongjin cursed, grabbed a woman—Shaw's wife—and dragged her away from the others, his AK-47 swinging all over the place.

"Let her go," Shaw growled. "Take me instead."

"Shut up! Listen to me, whoever you are, I will not hesitate to kill them all. I'm walking out of here."

As if, Wallace thought, that would convince the invaders. If Chongjin was a reasonable man he could see the error of his ways. Right then he couldn't see them, as they grabbed cover, but he could imagine Chongjin— and his own mug—were lined up in crosshairs. And all of them standing out in the open like this, ringed by all manner of cover the attackers could take.

Wallace took in the numbers, then gave Pender the nod. Slowly his men took a few paces away from the North Korean soldiers. Including Chongjin, he was looking at nine guys. And the North Koreans, eyes darting all around, were more concerned about the hidden gunmen.

It looked like no better opportunity to turn the tables and go for himself. Confusion and fear all around, Chongjin thinking that maybe Wallace and his guys were really only there to help out.

He was about to help, all right.

Himself.

SHAW READ THE HORROR in his wife's eyes, her expression searching him out, it seemed, silently begging him to do something—or at least save himself and his daughter somehow. Fear and cold rage swelled his limbs, and he took a step forward. Unsure what he was going to do, but he wasn't about to watch her get murdered.

"No further, Mr. Shaw!"

Shaw stopped, then noticed the Americans were circling outside the North Koreans. Something dark and ominous had clouded their eyes, and he suspected what would happen next. He pulled Patti to him, ready to throw his daughter to the floor, charge the colonel and take a bullet for his wife if that's what it came down to.

Then he saw the Americans turn their weapons on Chongjin's soldiers. A nod from the one he believed was called Wallace and all hell broke loose.

THE EXECUTIONER saw it coming.

Bolan was hunkered beside a crate, sensing the rising tide of panic some thirty feet away.

It was poised to go to hell.

Chongjin spun his human shield in his direction, as if instinctively locking in on Bolan's presence. The soldier flicked his selector shot mode to single-fire and lifted the M-16. One bullet straight for the head would do the trick.

The Americans were going to start a slaughter. They were jacked up on their fear and a selfish desire to make it out of there no matter what. It was going to be close, and hopefully the hostages would hit the deck out of terror.

CHONGJIN SQUEEZED Shaw's wife tighter to his chest. It was awkward, wrestling the AK-47, but it wouldn't take much effort to shove her ahead, shoot her in the back and then kill the others.

That included Wallace.

Wait a second! How did the four mercs get themselves into a ring outside his own men?

"You bastards!"

The dream was dead. He saw the end like a mighty explosion going off. Betrayed at every corner. The council. Kim Jong Il.

The rage exploded like a bomb in his gut.

Chongjin pushed the woman away and was swinging the assault rifle around, lining it up on her spine when he glimpsed a tall figure in black rise from behind a crate. A single wink of flame and then there was blackness.

CHONGJIN DROPPED, the back of his skull flying away. The woman screamed as a man reached out, grabbed her and threw her to the floor. It was one 5.56 mm slug from Bolan's rifle right between the colonel's eyes.

Well, the first shot was easy. Bolan was already flicking the mode back to full-auto.

His team was spread around the circle of crates. Bolan caught the tops of their heads, assault rifles already out and flaming. Whoever the Americans were, more thugs for the Phoenix Council he reckoned, they unleashed concentrated barrages of autofire on the North Korean soldiers. As hoped for, the hostages began knocking each other to the floor, men covering the heads of women as the storm blew over them. The NK soldiers didn't stand a chance.

Between Bolan's concentrated lethal barrage, one clean head shot after another of Chongjin's soldiers, and his Alpha team snapping off precision bursts, the ring of NK shooters was nearly down and out as soon as the black-ops mercs went berserk. They were twitching around, screaming and firing wild bursts still toward the ceiling.

The immediate problem was the SDI scientist Bolan recognized from the intel pics as Shaw. The man had already grabbed his daughter, flinging her down, his other arm covering his wife's head. The autofire was blazing all around the hostages, all of whom had dropped, holding on as blood showers rained down on them.

Bolan couldn't get a line on the four mercs who had turned their weapons on the North Koreans. The dancing dead actually provided protection for the hardmen, long enough for one of them to haul in another human shield. Beyond the snapping of bullets, Bolan heard him shouting something to the other three. They might have looked silly and awkward in their prisoner coveralls, but they sure enough had the weapons, tenacity, and now were seeking to desperately grab another edge.

More hostages.

15

Somehow Wallace found himself still standing, in one piece, all body parts functioning. No holes pumping out blood. Somehow he'd missed getting shot, by inches or less, his ears still buzzing with any number of rounds that had snapped past while he stood his ground and mowed down Chongjin's soldiers with his own men hanging right in there, getting it done. Since he'd been shot in the past, he knew what to look for in that regard—burning, racing from scalp to toe. He was drenched in blood, of course, but all the sticky red juices came from the bodies of Chongjin's boys who were on the floor now, down and twitching out.

And he had a nice little wall of human flesh around him. Covered for the moment.

Or was he?

"I know you're out there. What are you? SEALs? Delta? I guess it doesn't matter, but here's the scoop. Same deal as Chongjin," he shouted, searching the crates, machinery, tool benches and the deepest shadows of the massive warehouse for any sign of encroachment. He listened to the silence, but heard only the soft cries of the hostages beneath him. He grabbed Shaw's wife tight to his chest—don't ask him how he pulled that move off—with all Chongjin's men going down or standing tall, holding on while taking bullets. He had managed to snap the lady back up, kick the husband in the jaw, while Pender grabbed the daughter, reeling in yet more human armor. As more good luck had it, Thompkins had snagged Monroe's wife, and Bide had the nicely put together Janet Miles in tow.

The best of the best, all around, he considered.

They were going to make it out, he could feel it, or the bullets would have already started flying again.

"Okay, nice and easy, we're backstroking out of here. Pull it in tighter, gentlemen," he told his men. "Nice ring, duckwalk, cover your knees, we move in a slow circle. Hey, any crap from you heroes and I can waste them all. I'm a tough bastard, you'll need to empty a whole clip into me. While you're doing that, I waste them all. Makes you showing up here a waste of time."

Where the hell were they? he wondered. No noise, not a scuffling of boots even.

He risked a look over his shoulder and saw the roll-up door beyond an aisle of crates.

Tough going, but there was no other way. Someone would have to open the door, which meant letting go of a shield to bend down. And if it was locked...

"You're taking me, too."

Now what? he thought, and found Shaw, blood running down the corner of his mouth from where Wallace had whacked him. His eyes were wild as he walked straight toward him. What was this? The geeky scientist was all of a sudden a tough guy?

"You want to come, Shaw, make sure the wife and girl make it, that's fine. Fall in, right in front of me. Anything cute, well, you know the drill. You've seen me work."

"Nothing cute."

"Good boy. I kind of like you anyway. You've shown some guts. Play it straight and everybody walks out of here."

"I understand."

"STAY COOL," Bolan whispered into the mouthpiece of his com-link, hooked into Alpha team on the same frequency. "They're heading for the back door. I'm going north to the wall, then west. I'll try to pinch them in your way, Tolley." He talked to his two blacksuits out back and confirmed their position in the lot where a few more vehicles were scattered about, the motor pool providing them cover for the coming sniping task. "Head shots. Four of them. On my word. No misses. It has to be done right first time out."

He heard the voice of the one of the hostages. He didn't like the tone. Shaw, the SDI scientist, was worried about his wife and daughter. It was aggressive to the point of reckless, but he heard the merc tell Shaw to get in, followed by a word of warning not to be a hero.

Bolan was rounding the corner of piled crates when

he saw one of the hardmen forced to give up his hold on a woman. He reached down and grabbed the handle to throw up the rolling door.

And then it went straight to hell once again.

THE THUG HE KNEW as Wallace took his eyes off him long enough for Shaw to try to save his wife and daughter. It was the craziest damn thing he'd ever done in his life, and if he survived, his wife and daughter unharmed, he would look back at this moment and wonder how in the world he'd found the nerve, guts or whatever to do something he would have never dreamed himself capable of. Maybe it was everything he'd endured, from being kidnapped on through, fraying him inside, snapping him now, urging to try and do anything he could to turn it all around.

He also got some help from Janet Miles.

Shaw lunged, wrapped his hands around the barrel of the AK-47 and shoved it up. The sudden move shocked Wallace, and the man lost his grip on his wife.

"Get down!" he hollered in the faces of Patti and his wife.

Wallace snarled curses and they started wrestling for control of the weapon. As his wife and daughter hit the floor, he glimpsed Miles slash an elbow over the jaw of the hardman behind her. It was a solid connection. The blow freed the woman. Turning, all anger and determination in her expression, Miles looked set to claw out the guy's eyes.

Shaw bellowed in outrage, fearing it was all over, his

one attempt to do something dramatic, to pull off the impossible was all for nothing as the blood spattered his face.

"DO IT!"

They were in perfect sync, capping off rounds, going for head shots. Two brave folks, a woman and Shaw, Bolan saw, had created an opening, giving him and Alpha team the only chance to take out the black-ops mercs.

It helped that the warehouse door was up, enabling his two Alpha shooters out back to aid in driving rounds through skulls. Once again the human armor was hitting the floor, getting out of the line of fire, all of them but Shaw and the woman, who appeared set to spear her fingers through her captor's eyes. Only half his skull vanished in the next microsecond, her face splattered, the gore shower driving her back. She cried out and hit her knees, either thinking she was hit perhaps or simply figuring out the play, her instinct for survival taking over. Whatever, she was down and out of the way.

Maybe ten shots were triggered by Alpha team; Bolan couldn't say. In the final analysis it didn't matter. They all connected, bullets driving through brain matter, punching out their lights in less than a heartbeat, the hardmen pitching this way and that. They slammed to the floor, convulsing in death throes, AK-47s slipping from lifeless fingers.

"We're clear in here!" Bolan told his shooters outside. "We're coming out!"

"Roger. We're clear out here, too, Striker."

Bolan gathered with Tolley and his Alpha shooters near the doorway. The hostages didn't need to be told the massacre was over, but the soldier suspected they might meet resistance outside. A call to the Delta Force leader, and he found there were still scattered pockets of armed resistance, but most of the North Koreans were running for the hills. Bolan then radioed his men out front. They were likewise clear, but they asked about the shooting over near the airfield, where whatever North Korean soldiers survived the bombardment were getting taken out by the Delta Force commandos. Bolan told them he was calling in the Sea Stallions. Delta had the situation under control.

"Everybody listen to me," Bolan told the group, searching their faces, taking a quick head count and coming up with fifteen. A few of them looked shaky, on the verge of collapsing under the strain, but it was understandable. Still, there was a light of hope in all their eyes. That was a definite plus. The taste of freedom was just around the corner. "We're going to form a ring around you. We're going out the back and will make our way to the front. I'm calling in our chopper now."

A man broke from the group—Monroe, he believed. He looked as if he was about to fall to his knees.

"Oh, thank you, whoever you are."

"We're not home free yet," Bolan told him.

"STRIKER to Behemoth One, come in."

Grimaldi was three miles out over the Haeju harbor,

circling the black waters in a long, looping run at ten thousand feet and holding, waiting to dive in there and do his thing. Six F-15s were flying cover two hundred feet up. It was quite the spectacle of death and destruction out there on the distant airfield, the air strike having laid waste to anything that could fly and threaten their own pilots, not to mention the lumbering Spectre would have proved a sitting duck if any of those MiGs had taken to the air.

It didn't happen. So far it was falling to plan. He noted the flurry of activity in the sub bunker and called the squadron leader of the F-15s. Apparently they were untying the sub now in a desperate attempt to save the ship. They were all waiting for the extraction to lower the final curtain of doom.

It was just about Grimaldi's turn to clean up.

"Behemoth One here, Striker."

"I've called in our ride. Give us ten minutes to clear out. I've got some hostiles near our extract site, then move in. It's your show. The sub bunker is Joy Ride's job. All of our people are present and accounted for. Chongjin and his Phoenix Council buddies won't rise from the ashes. Touch back with Joy Ride and get the last two strikes meshed so we don't get sucked in by the firestorm on the way out. Copy."

"Aye, aye, Striker. I'm on the clock."

The big building to the distant north was pegged by intelligence as a combo nuke-waste reprocessing plant and missile-building facility. According to the CIA, the North Koreans were close to manufacturing a dozen

ICBMs there, but they had fallen behind schedule getting them fitted with the megaton punch. It was still their pride and joy.

It was history.

Of course, Grimaldi would have to get some more altitude, just in case something with a little more wallop— like a small nuke—was touched off.

Ah, the hell with it. For once he was going to trust that their own intelligence people had it right. It was a waste-reprocessing plant, with missiles not yet fitted with the necessary radioactive packages to give an ICBM the kind of muscle required to vaporize a city or two.

They'd find out soon enough.

Grimaldi turned and gave his crew the thumbs-up. "Let's tighten up, gentlemen. We're on deck."

WHEN THE EXECUTIONER and Tolley led the hostages around the west edge of Building A, he found his black-suits under fire from the North Koreans hunkered both inside the doorways and in the trio of concrete bunkers that led to the sub dock belowground.

The motor pool, he found, had also been torched to flaming trash. Obviously a runner had chosen flight over fight. The standing order from Bolan had been to blow it all if even one rabbit tried to bolt.

An overturned Humvee, smoking, but with flames dying out, was providing his two blacksuits with temporary cover. Bolan judged the angle to the bunkers, figured a few well-placed 40 mm missiles should do it if they squeezed them through the openings just right.

Figure three to five feet to spare to slip the bombs through and they had the LZ to themselves.

"All of you," he told the hostages, "hug the wall of this building and wait until I tell you it's clear."

Nods all around, and the soldier sensed they were more than eager to comply with any orders given them.

Then Bolan told his teammates what he wanted for the big bang. He handed out individual bunker assignments to make sure they got them all in one flash.

Their Sea Stallion pickup was three minutes away, and the soldier needed the LZ swept of hostiles.

With a 40 mm bomb down the M-203's barrel, Bolan and company hit their knees, a skirmish line of missile men, shoulder to shoulder.

"Let it rip," the Executioner ordered.

And the salvo of missiles chugged out. It was bull's-eye down the line. The flaming assault rifles from those concrete cubbyholes were silenced by the sweeping blasts.

Bolan took a sitrep from his blacksuits out front. A few moments later, as they checked the killzone on all points, the soldier got an all-clear.

He checked his watch. The clock was winding down. Bolan told everyone to move out, but for the hostages to stay inside their ring.

And Grimaldi, he knew, was getting antsy to lend his hand.

Bolan checked the flaming lake of twisted wreckage, bodies strewed in front of the building. Nothing but fire everywhere he looked, billowing mountains of smoke.

And the dead, strewed and mangled for as far as he could see.

He led the group of hostages and blacksuits to an area beyond the last of the wreckage. He was checking the roofline of Building A, feeling something wasn't quite right, closing on his blacksuits when one of them said, "What have we got here, sir?"

The black van was slowly riding in from the east. It was lit up by the raging firestorms swirling over the airfield.

And clearly framing the faces of two North Koreans in the van.

Bolan stepped away from the group, ordered Tolley to come with him and told his blacksuits to keep the hostages secured and moving to the south. He expected more trouble. And he hadn't come this far to see this rescue mission fail.

The van stopped, the driver and passenger doors opening. Quickly Bolan reloaded the M-203 and fed a new clip to his assault rifle. They weren't waving white flags, but two men rolled out in long dark topcoats, their hands held high above their heads.

The side door slid back next and two more North Koreans, both armed with assault rifles, stepped outside.

"Can we talk?" one of them called out.

16

Something smelled real bad to Bolan.

And it wasn't all the burning fuel, running blood or loosed bowels and bladders from dead men. All those cloying stinks of war he had known and grown accustomed to.

The Executioner felt ambush in the air, and they weren't fooling him in the least.

The men were side by side now, he saw, keeping the assault rifles low by their legs. It was an act on their part, he was sure of it, attempting to get him to think they were there—for what? Extend an olive branch? All's forgiven?

Not hardly, Bolan knew. But where was the threat? He was anxious to be on his way, but a part of him couldn't wait to hear what kind of con game they wanted to play on him. No sense in leaving behind any loose ends. They were operatives out of Pyongyang, Kim Jong Il's thugs. What were a few more enemy bodies at this point anyway?

"Nothing to talk about. Have a nice night," Bolan said. "Give Kim Jong Il our regards."

"Wait! You have what you want. The American hostages are going home. I am assuming Chongjin and the rest of his renegade army has been wiped out."

"You assume right."

"That's a good thing."

"I see, that's your way of thanking me."

"Not quite."

"Really? You know, from where you stand, I think you should be thanking us for cleaning up your mess in your own backyard."

"I am not standing here prepared to grovel."

"Have a nice life."

"Hold on, please!"

Bolan was turning away but stopped. They were starting to annoy him, and he was wondering when it was going to blow.

"You have given us what you would call payback, yes, plenty of it. Pyongyang regrets what happened in your country, the loss of your special aircraft, your countrymen dying at the hands of terrorists. No mistake, we consider Colonel Chongjin a terrorist. No one will mourn his passing. However, I am here to bring one request to you from our president."

Bolan felt the hair rising on the back of his neck, some menace out there, closing in.

"Quickly."

"Spare the nuclear facility. Spare the submarine bunker. They are invaluable to our nation's defense. They have taken much time and considerable expense simply to get them built and operating and even we have not fully completed our work at the facility."

"I consider that a good thing."

"I'm thinking you are saving them for last. Please rethink that. In time our countries can work out our differences, patch up the unfortunate misunderstanding, all the trouble that was brought on by one man."

"I'm not a politician," Bolan said. "This place is finished, all of it. I suggest you ride away, as far as you can before you become another casualty."

"Please, be reasonable."

Bolan heard his com-link crackle to life. "Sniper Team Leader to Striker, you've got a problem on the roof. It's a setup."

The Executioner whirled toward Building A and spotted the two armed shadows near the edge, but they were already getting nailed by the Delta snipers, dark stick figures lifted off their feet and sent flying out of sight.

"Don't!" the North Korean roared, throwing out his hands as if that would save him from the coming hail of lead.

Spinning back toward the North Koreans, Bolan took the lead in dishing it out, holding back on the M-16's trigger. Tolley pitched in, his M-16 chattering in unison. The hardmen were raising their assault rifles, but Bolan drove them into each other with a long burst of autofire across their chests. Swinging his aim back, he found Tolley had the men pinned to the side of the van, spasming, cut to red ruins. Bolan threw in a few rounds, nailing it down, watching them crumple and slide down the van's side, jerking around in death throes on the ground.

Bolan keyed the com-link frequency to his snipers. "Striker to Sniper Team Leader, how do we look now?"

"I'll keep watch on your backs until pickup, but you look clear."

Bolan signed off, one eye on the roofline just the same, as he rolled for the LZ. He looked at his watch and he knew Grimaldi was en route for some massive mopping up. In the East he spotted one of the Sea Stallions already picking up Delta Force, right on time, then lifting off for the ridgeline to retrieve their snipers.

The Executioner rejoined the freed captives and his blacksuits. He spotted the dark bulk of their own chopper ride sweeping down over the ridgeline for pickup.

Time to go home, Bolan thought, and gave the sweeping wasteland a final search. Or at least back to friendly turf.

SHAW LISTENED to his wife and daughter quietly sob as they collapsed together on a seat or bench or whatever it was. He didn't care where he sat or on what; they were going home. The helicopter was lifting off. For a second, the relief was so overwhelming he thought he might be sick. He felt his wife throw her arms around him and squeeze, her hot tears running down his cheek.

"Thomas, you were very brave back there."

"I had to do something. I was tired of doing nothing. I want you to know I love you. I want you to know there are some things about me that have changed because of all of this. I can't quite explain it now, but in due time, you will see it."

"I believe you. I think you've seen something in yourself that's maybe caused our family some quiet suffering over the years."

"You and my girls will become the absolute focal point of my life from here on."

He kissed her, stroking her hair, then pulled back and began whispering soothing words to his daughter that it was over, they would be home soon.

The big guy in charge, he saw, was standing near the doorway, watching the vast sea of fire and destruction that had been their very temporary prison. It looked as if he was waiting for some final drama or conflagration, the intensity in those cold blue eyes mounting as he checked his watch. All around in the chopper Shaw heard them making sounds of joy, laughter barely subdued, sounding giddy as men and women hugged each other and sobbed in joy.

Who was the big man? he wondered. A black-ops expert of some sort, no doubt, a savior, to be sure, but Shaw would never even know his name. And if he did? What would he do, he laughed to himself, send a Christmas card or invite him over for dinner? But because of him and the other blacksuits, the nightmare was over. And that was all that really mattered. He could sift through the pieces later, try to reason out what had happened—why them and why this ordeal?—then figured why bother?

It was more than enough to see his family safe and by his side.

In the final analysis, he thought, it didn't get any better than this.

Freedom, and life, were precious, something to cherish and hold on to and never take for granted.

Just like his family.

THEY WERE SOARING high above the ridgeline of the cliff overlooking the harbor when Grimaldi and the

Spectre crew unloaded on the North Koreans' prized nuclear-waste reprocessing and missile-building facility. Their dreams of becoming a nuclear superpower got the full Spectre treatment, trampling their desire to become nuclear gods.

It was pounded all to hell in less than thirty seconds as the flying battleship sailed on, covered by the fighter jets, all guns and cannons flaming and booming out the message of vengeance. The whole facility went up, the cooling tower vanishing in a towering fireball that made Bolan briefly wonder how irradiated and for long this stretch of North Korea would be left in the aftermath.

Final payback.

No blinding mushroom cloud boiled up, but the fire seemed to take on some sort of brilliant sheen, as radioactive waste and water were hurled into the firestorm, rocket fuel igniting to add another hellish dimension. There were shadows still, running pell-mell in the distance, he spotted, quickly shrinking to his sight, and he forgot about them. There wouldn't be enough pieces of whoever was left standing.

It was good to see it go up in flames. It wouldn't bring back all the innocent American dead, but sometimes, sad but true, vengeance was all that was left, Bolan thought.

Moments later, as the Sea Stallion pushed fast and hard across the harbor, Bolan looking up and spotted their own trio of Tomcats prepared to escort them back to Dujan. He spotted the nose of the *Kim Jong Il* nuclear sub poking out of the bunker. Whether it was moving out, he couldn't tell, since a few moments later it disappeared in a fireball. More high-tech laser-guided missiles then plunged into the conflagration, just to make sure, some of the SAMs hammering the cliff above the gaping entrance to bring down a wall of rock that would take a whole lot of effort just to clear away before for the North Koreans could get inside and even begin to assess the damage.

It was very doubtful that there was anything left in that mess to salvage.

The Executioner looked away from the last firestorm. He'd seen enough.

"I JUST CAME to check on you, see how you're managing. I know it's been pure hell on you and your family, but you can expect to be well taken care of, compensated by our government for your ordeal. That came straight from my boss, Mr. Shaw."

Bolan was in their private quarters at Dujan. Shaw's wife and daughter, exhausted by their nightmare, were asleep in their bunks. It was over for the fifteen Americans, but Bolan still had work to do back in the States. He had touched base with Brognola as soon as he had landed at the CIA base, and the big Fed was hard at work ironing out logistics to get himself, Tolley and Grimaldi to several waiting hot zones where the final army of the Phoenix Council had been identified and located.

Shaw rose and held out his hand. Bolan took it.

"I don't know what to say, except thank you."

Bolan nodded. The man was shaking, but he was

holding up, his stare brimming with gratitude and relief. The man might have been a civilian scientist and not a soldier with combat experience and blood on his hands, but he was a warrior in his own right. He had shown remarkable courage in the warehouse, and right then the soldier knew his family was all that mattered to him.

The sweet bliss of freedom after captivity, and Bolan allowed him a moment of silence to enjoy it, even in his presence.

"You'll be going home in a few hours. I can't say exactly how long you'll have to remain here. You'll get a change of clothes, get cleaned up and you'll be well fed. There will be a short delay, a debriefing and a medical examination."

"I understand. Any place is better than where we were."

"Good luck to you."

"Same to you. And thanks again."

They shook again, and Bolan turned and left the man to his family.

Bolan was tired, whipped to the bone himself, the strain of the hell miles adding up, taking their toll. There would be a little time to rest during the flight back to the States, but he had a lot to do in the meantime, plans to sort out, a strategy to put into place. He wanted names and locations nailed down.

Places to go, people to visit.

The Executioner had snakes and rats back in the States to hunt down and crush. It would take some time getting back, with Tolley making some last-minute arrangements to get all the other blacksuits in place, but Bolan could hardly wait to put the final cleansing flame to a bunch of traitors who had brought more hell and horror into the world than he could recall in a long time.

For somebody in hiding, the payback was about to begin.

17

It was a big desert out there inside the Nevada border, but the NSA's head of security for the so-called Area 20 felt the walls closing in, the air hot and stifling despite the air-conditioning cranked up to full blast in the diner. It could have been the six cups of coffee heating up his blood, and all the caffeine sure wasn't doing much to calm Michael Sellers's jittery nerves, either. He considered spiking it with some whiskey.

Not this night.

He needed full and complete control of his faculties. There was trouble all over the map, and no one was able to pin down exactly who was kicking up the storm from the States all the way into North Korea, much less where trouble would drop out of the sky next.

Almost all of their contacts and connections had been severed overseas, just for starters, and he wasn't thinking about a simple disconnect of a phone line. Someone had declared war on the council and it looked as if they—whoever they were—were winning. If the violent dismantling of their infrastructure went on much longer, it sure as hell looked as though the dream of taking over the country by chemical and biological extortion was down the toilet.

While he waited on the man for the delivery of this month's cash allotment and ostensibly further orders from back east, he pondered the crisis that was on the verge of bringing the entire Phoenix Council—or what was left of it—to its knees.

First Tolley, the DIA traitor, had fled to points unknown, months of tracking the man ending in a bloody fiasco for a team of black-ops warriors from the council, and those guys had been no second-string talent. The reported body count alone from the murderous debacle in the California desert boggled his mind. Apparently Tolley had mined his shack and slipped out somehow while the black-ops team hit the steps, ready to kick the door down and go in, guns blazing. Pressure plates on both front and back stoops. Sneaky bastard.

At least that was the report he got from Irwin. It came complete with alarm bells sounding about a gunship that had been used to blow up everything—vehicles and bodies blasted off the face of the desert. If that was the case, someone—another black-ops team—was onto them, betrayed by the surviving members of the council to either stab them in the back at this crisis point or...

Or were they hitters sanctioned to hunt them down via orders from the White House?

It happened.

Which made him worry all the more.

Then there was the bloody mystery of Port Moresby. Their Doomsday Army, a hundred-plus men he had helped to seek out, recruit and ship to the jungle outpost up the Fly River in Papua New Guinea, had been wiped out by some sort of combined air-ground attack. Then— if he could believe what he heard coming out of PNG from their two remaining sets of eyes and ears over there—a two-man wrecking crew had blown through Port Moresby, taking out their bagmen, politicians and bankers under the council's command and direction.

PNG was a wash, a total loss, with what few power players they had left in the shadows scrambling to cover their own assets and pointing fingers of blame wherever they could or simply cleaning out bank accounts and fleeing for God only knew where.

And the nameless, faceless attackers who had torn like a hurricane through Port Moresby had just vanished, leaving behind more ruins for the council to sift through, more mystery to ponder and agonize over.

There was also the not so little headache over the disappearance of the charter members of the council, rumored to have either been abducted by Colonel Chongjin or perhaps having gone willingly with the North Koreans when it hit the fan in Oklahoma. No backbone on the part of those men to stay behind and take their chances like the rest of them. There were reports, coming from his source in Washington, that their North Korean subcontractors had their compound in Haeju blown off the map during a government-sanctioned surgical strike.

Well, the brigadier general, his cronies and black-ops men back in Washington didn't have a clue. They weren't talking, pretty much hinting, "Don't call us— we'll call you."

All of it left him in the dark, thrashing around inside with worry about tomorrow, wondering if he shouldn't just cash in his own chips, pack up a few of his men, grab one of the Gulfstreams they'd used to fly recruits to PNG and bail.

He was considering doing just that, after this night, when the deliveryman came, dumped off their money and melted back into the night. The deliveries alone were another problem to brood over. They always sent a different cutout.

Sellers gave his crew a look. Eight black-ops warriors were strung out down the counter. The diner belonged to them, the owner fairly aware of who and what they were, but they greased him with enough cash to make sure he stayed deaf, dumb and blind. He gave them the run of the place during after-hours for these clandestine meets. If some sort of trouble did rear up, there was always enough firepower in the diner. They were all packing Glocks in shoulder rigging, with Uzis and MP-5s on the countertop. He started thinking about the guys from Irwin again, wondering if maybe he should have brought the other ten ops along for the meet. But the director of Area 20 didn't see the necessity to march out the entire security detail for the rendezvous with one man when he needed some armed guards on hand to watch the store. Maybe the director knew more about all the trouble finding the council than he was letting on?

Well, that was a bureaucrat for you, Sellers thought. He was keeping something to himself, or maybe he'd marched all of them out there while he raided some hidden safe packed with the council's cash then grabbed one of the Gulfstreams while they weren't looking.

Sellers was downing another swig of coffee when his tac radio crackled. He punched on and listened to Mathers. His sentry was patrolling the grounds around the diner.

"Sir, I've got a vehicle coming in from the northwest. One occupant."

He was driving in from the northwest, when they were sitting with their backs to the plate-glass window, watching the southern expanse of open desert. They always knew to come in from the south, so why the change in the program? He was coming in from their blind side at the moment, Sellers thought, or was paranoia getting the best of him?

"Keep me posted, and watch those hills. Out.

"Look alive, gentlemen, the council's delivery boy is here."

THE EXECUTIONER HAD already reconned what he could of the squat, block-shaped building after making his way down a gully in the northern hills, pulling up forty or so yards away to watch the sentry. Two GMCs were out front. There was one sentry roving the premises, sticking close to the foothills, looking around, smoking. With all the open desert to the south and east, there was no way Bolan could have surveyed the place from that direction and get any fix on enemy numbers without being seen.

It was better this way, he reckoned, coming in from their back side. They'd bulldoze the action, both of them locking the enemy in a lightning pincers attack inside the diner. Figure eight, ten men tops, and he was going in the back door while Tolley went in through the front. Bolan had warned Tolley they might recognize him as the DIA man the late Irwin black-ops platoon had been hunting and open fire on sight. But Tolley insisted on doing it his way, that if they knew who he was, there would be a moment of shock during which Bolan could come out of the kitchen and let them have it from behind.

Fine.

The plan was already worked out with Tolley in advance. Bolan had agreed that the man had a point about the strike itself. Shock factor might pull it off, men freezing up while Bolan started sweeping them from behind with his M-16.

They'd find out soon enough, within two minutes by his judgment.

The call was put in a few hours ago and the rendezvous was arranged. According to Tolley, they were black-ops men from a small installation just to the south where the weapons of mass destruction for the Doomsday Army had been manufactured. Grimaldi was also parked a few miles to the south in his Cobra gunship. Nellis had been taken over two days ago by a team of Justice and FBI agents handpicked by Brognola. Since it was in the neighborhood of his enemies and the two strikes planned, Bolan decided to use Nellis Range as his temporary base of operations.

Bolan was there now, moving in for the kill, the sound-suppressed Beretta 93-R out and taking aim.

It had been a long plane ride from overseas, then another shuttle layover at Nellis, Bolan briefly reflected, to get to this point where he could begin the final clean sweep of the surviving savages of the Phoenix Council. He reckoned more than forty hours since finally flying from Dujan, and between layovers, he waited on Brognola and the Farm to get him the necessary satellite imagery of the council's Nevada installation and to further check out the facts on Tolley's story about the black-ops program inside the Nevada border with California.

He was a second away from burning down another rat's nest, taking up slack on the trigger. The lookout had been more keenly intent on watching Tolley drive in than concentrating on some ghost sliding through the night, then he started to turn toward the shadow closing in on his back side.

Way too late to come alive now.

Bolan dropped him with a head shot, then began making his way for the back door. As soon as Tolley parked, ready to step out and walk up to the front door, Bolan would give the signal to go through his throat mike.

The Executioner leathered the Beretta and unslung the M-16.

TOLLEY ANGLED the SUV they'd taken from Nellis in front of the glass window, close enough to the door so it wouldn't take but a few steps to barge inside before they knew what was hitting them. Eight heads were turning his way, but his face was in the dark for the moment.

Soon enough, he hoped, they'd recognize the face of

the man they'd been hunting since he'd bailed the DIA and given the council the middle-finger salute.

And there was a good chance they'd know who he was, but by the time he was in the doorway, his M-16 would be up and spitting lead, cranking it out.

He also knew he might die. So far he'd gotten lucky, or fighting beside Belasko had given him enough of an edge to get by. In a way he didn't care if he saw the night out. Something had changed inside him after North Korea, a dark emptiness that kept spreading and swelling his soul. The long flight back to Nevada hadn't done much to calm some stirring demon in his belly, in fact, and thinking about his life only made it worse. He figured he knew what it was that was eating him up. After his business was finished with Belasko, he would have nothing to live for. Belasko would go on, doing what he did, hunting down the world's scum, while he drifted off into obscurity, drinking the days away, wondering where his life had gone.

It was a victory, of sorts, that he'd convinced Belasko to let him go through the front door, while the man went through the kitchen. It would be his last grandstand play if it worked out the way he wanted.

He had helped Belasko all he could, and soon he would be eased out of the picture when his services were no longer required. Yes, all of his intel on the council had checked out, but whoever Belasko worked for—and Tolley was no fool, the Justice Department was itself running some sort of black-ops program—had verified certain facts. Satellite imagery of Area 20 had confirmed his intel. Since Belasko had received the go-ahead from his boss after the call to set up the rendezvous, the two GMCs out front had been monitored by satellite as they pulled out of the installation where the weapons of mass destruction had been produced. It meant the rendezvous was on, and it once again told Belasko he was telling the truth.

Tolley was ready to go for it again, maybe for the last time, his heart racing, adrenaline burning.

He bent over, away from their watching eyes, acting as if he was grabbing something, and whispered into his throat mike, "I'm going in." He checked the illuminated dial of his watch, then gauged the few steps to the door. "Thirty seconds and counting."

He was stretching the time, but Belasko didn't need to know that.

He took his M-16 and opened the door, the light bulb already smashed out before he drove up. He kept the M-16 hidden as best he could by his leg. A quick glance inside the diner and he saw their bodies tensing, then hands reaching for holstered weapons.

Tolley walked over and flung open the door. He saw them freeze on their stools, eyes wide in recognition, just as expected. "Yes, it's me, gentlemen, Tolley, slayer of black-ops demons!" He laughed, lifting his assault rifle.

Tolley held back on the trigger and began blasting.

IT WAS JUST the moment since PNG that Bolan knew had been coming on.

Tolley had lost it, plunged over the edge in some suicidal last stand.

The Executioner was through the back door, weaving his way through the kitchen, past the stainless-steel prep counter. Tolley was out there, screaming and shooting up the place. A quick look through the window of the swing door and Bolan found the man, standing in the front doorway, his M-16 blazing.

He was also taking hits, his stomach erupting in shredded cloth and flesh, blood spraying his face as the hardmen held their ground by the counter and hit him with everything they had.

The Executioner had no choice but to bull his way into the action. He went through the door and began hosing them down the line. It was a full-auto sweep, the soldier's barrage of 5.56 mm lead shattering skulls, kicking the hardmen away from the counter, their pistols and subguns briefly chattering on as they toppled. Bolan moved away from the door, firing on the run and dropping two more with head blasts.

The Executioner had no time to ponder the sudden madness that gripped Tolley. Shooters were turning his way. One was breaking for the door, triggering a Glock as fast as he could, his firing hasty, flinging bullets all around in a blind panic.

Bolan felt the hot lead singe his scalp, but his barrage was already eating up their chests, driving them away from their stools.

The runner pumped two rounds into Tolley, who finally pitched backward through the doorway. Bolan stepped away from the counter as the hardman wheeled, bringing the Glock up.

Bolan drilled him with a figure eight, slamming him

into the door frame, where he bounced and crashed to the floor.

The Executioner looked at the strewed bodies, trying to detect any signs of life. He gave the carnage a walk-through, toeing bodies, watching for any telltale flicker in empty stares.

It was a wrap there.

And Tolley was finished.

The soldier stood over the DIA man. It was pointless to feel for a pulse, but Bolan did it anyway.

Tolley was gone.

Bolan shook his head, wondering what had gone through the man's mind in his last moments. He didn't have to throw it all away like this.

Later, Bolan may or may not wonder, and perhaps even feel some gratitude for the help Tolley had given him. Right then the soldier had to take down a factory that had produced weapons of mass destruction.

Bolan plucked up his tac radio to call in Grimaldi.

18

One flyover of the factory by the Cobra had them barreling out the front door near the main gate, Bolan saw, subguns waving around, men yelling up at the night sky as if the gunship was supposed to drop down, its pilot hop out and simply surrender.

As if it was all some big mistake.

It was, Bolan decided.

Theirs.

The building itself wasn't much in terms of size or sophistication from what he could see, a gray, nondescript concrete block with one giant satellite dish on the roof, the compound ringed by cyclone fence. Planted near the foot of some barren hills on a broken plateau, the building wasn't much larger than nine or ten town homes thrown together in a square, but Bolan had to believe there were sleeping quarters and a command-and-control center in the guts of the building, as well as the work area where the poison had—or still was—manufactured belowground.

It was big enough, judging from all the fifty-gallon

drums piled against the building, near the lone eighteen-wheeler. And they were stamped with the skull and crossbones, either toxic waste or whatever precursor agents stored in the barrels that were necessary to create the poison the Doomsday Army would have used to hold entire American cities hostage.

The Executioner had no intention of going inside and risking exposure to deadly nerve gas or some genetically engineered super bio agent. No, they were driving the snakes out of their nest by smoke and fire. Cleanup would be left to more of Brognola's HAZMAT people.

Bolan took up his sniping roost on a ledge, sixty yards due west, looking directly down at the motor pool of SUVs and jeeps. The plan was straightforward—blow them up and blast them to hell, and this blitz was launched by Grimaldi. The barrels added a new dimension, a definite problem if there was a stray rocket.

Hell with it. They were there; they'd gone this far. No point in pulling punches now.

The Cobra's rocket pods, restocked at Nellis, began firing missiles, slamming the front wall. Grimaldi was coordinating the fireworks with a tenacious pounding by the 20 mm cannon. Start bringing down the roof.

Going in, the Stony Man warriors intended this lightning assault to let the movers and shakers of mass death know in their last moments that their death shop was closed for business for good.

Again no prisoners.

If they played true to form, as he had seen so many of the council's lackeys, pawns, cutouts and mercenaries when the sky fell on them, shock and panic would get them scurrying to abandon the sinking ship and bolt for anything that would get them the hell away from there. By now Bolan had to believe word had surely spread about the series of disasters that had crushed the other members of the Phoenix Council.

They would run for their lives.

They did.

Grimaldi held the Cobra in its hovering position, maintaining a hundred-foot distance beyond and above the main gate. He kept hammering the building, strafing it, left to right, top to bottom with more rocket fire. Men were shouting and shaking their fists, flailing around in the dust bowl kicked up by the Cobra's rotorwash, a few of them ducking as debris flew over their heads or slammed into them, kicking them off their feet before they gathered their senses and stood again. Chunks of the building were being lost quickly in thundering fireballs as Grimaldi went on vandalizing the structure. A few of the men tried to hold their ground, firing subguns at the gunship, as if they had a hope in hell.

But someone in the storm showed some sense of self-preservation. He was tugging at men and flapping his arms at the gunship, a gesture that was almost comical considering the circumstances.

Eleven men had come out and they began heading for the motor pool as anticipated. All but one of them, a guy in a suit, was armed. Grimaldi shifted his aim and started hammering the vehicles with cannon fire.

That got their attention again as they skidded nearly

as a group, dropping and covering their heads as wreckage blew their way.

At that comparable arm's-length distance to his marks, with the lights hung from the fence and the motor pool going up in flames, illuminating the building and its grounds, no scope was required for Bolan to line up the rats. An expert sniper, it was home runs with each squeeze of the trigger. Before they realized five were down from head shots, Grimaldi had the gunship parked over the flaming lake of the motor pool as gas tanks ignited and men started running for the front gate.

Bolan was up and charging hard to head them off at the main gate. There were a few Gulfstreams to the east. They were crazy with panic and terror if they thought they'd get them airborne.

Bolan tagged two more as they bolted through the open main gate. He hit the M-16's trigger again and kicked another hardman off his feet.

That left three, and the last shooters were stumbling over broken ground, the man in the suit struggling to break into a sprint before his foot clipped some uneven patch of ground and he was on his face.

Bolan marched on, feeling mean, jacked up on adrenaline, M-16 tracking. The hardmen were swinging subguns around as they suddenly became aware they were being hunted for extinction. They appeared dazed by the entire lightning ferocity of the attack, hesitating at the sight of the soldier stepping through the thinning dust storm, looking amazed for a heartbeat that they were being gunned down by one shooter.

With his M-16 stuttering, the Executioner zipped them over the chest, knocking them in tandem to their backs.

"Who are you? What do you want? Why are you doing this?"

The man in the suit staggered to his feet, his hands up, trying to deal his way out, maybe.

"The Phoenix Council's finished. We're putting up the Closed sign on your poison factory. You're out of business."

"Wh-what... Look, all I was...I'm with the Department of Defense.... You can't do this...." The man must have read the look in Bolan's eyes and knew he was as dead as the others, as anger and defiance hardened his face. "Do you know what you've done here? Do you know we were on the verge of seizing the entire country, of restoring law and order to this land...do you—?"

"I know all about it," the Executioner said, and pulled the trigger.

The soldier and Grimaldi gave it a few minutes, as something flammable inside the rubble blew and touched off a firestorm that gathered raging strength within thirty seconds. If there were any more rats left inside, they had a choice to come running into Bolan's gun or be incinerated.

No rats.

A hand signal from the soldier and Grimaldi brought the Cobra in for a landing. No sense in standing around any longer while toxic waste or worse was dumped out of those drums. It was another mess for Brognola's people to clean up, but the soldier could be sure there was more toxic waste to get spilled.

Human waste.

"THE MAN AGONIZED over this long and hard, guys, but I just got the word. No prisoners. This is it, the big one. It will be as hush-hush as the North Korean strike. Only word is starting to leak out to the press. At any rate, that doesn't necessarily include taking out the four senators who are holed up there. They're dirty as they come, yes, and after all the lives that have been lost...the Man says he'll deal with any backlash on his end, but this one's going to get swept under the rug as best they can at the White House. Green light, gloves off. You've taken it this far—he says it's your show from here on out. Whatever it takes to mop up what's left of this Phoenix Council that we know of. However, if the senators want to surrender...well, it's your call, Striker. It's an armed fortress out there. DOD, NSA and DIA black-ops, countersurveillance, intelligence, all of them, dirty rat bastards, traitors of the worst kind who helped engineer the slaughter of our own citizens. According to our satellite and aerial recon and the size of the motor pool, there could be as many as twenty black-ops turncoats sitting on their political stooges."

It was more than twenty-four hours since Bolan and Grimaldi burned down the factory in Nevada. A number of developments, all of them bad, had been dumped in Bolan's lap since then. Brognola's Justice team had been shadowing a few of the more notable faces that

Tolley's intel had turned up since the soldier first laid eyes on the late DIA man. Four senators, one Marine brigadier general and his team of counterintelligence operatives from the Pentagon had been AWOL for several days. The senators had been nailed as coconspirators, thanks to their tawdry antics caught on film from out Hollywood way, and it didn't matter if they were being forced to do the council's bidding or not. They had made their choice as far as Bolan was concerned. Even if they were only council puppets, they had still betrayed their oath of office.

It was only several hours ago when a Justice team had watched on roving surveillance as the last of the final four, Senator Childs from Illinois, was removed by an American and a North Korean from his home in Great Falls. From there Brognola's people followed them to the Winchester, Virginia, estate of Brigadier General Martin. Quite the lineup of traitors was now hunkered down under Martin's roof. Bolan was going after every last of them. If the senators wanted to be cuffed, fine. If they armed themselves, he'd shoot them down just like any other savage enemy.

"I'll call you when it's over, Hal."

There was a heavy pause on the other end of the sat link. Bolan glanced up and saw the grim set to Grimaldi's features. They were in the fuselage of the OH-58 Kiowa JetRanger. While riding out the day, waiting on the green light, Brognola had moved their base of operations to a private airfield in Loudon County that was sometimes used by his agents, the

Farm pitching in to help set the table. With the added payload of TOW antitank missiles, coupled with the firepower of the 7.62 mm minigun, the big Fed had logistically put them as close to the target as possible without Grimaldi having to worry about redlining it all the way back.

Assuming, Bolan knew, they took care of business in Winchester.

"Good luck to both of you, and Godspeed," Brognola said. "Nail it down. I'll see you on the other side."

And Brognola signed off.

Grimaldi whistled. "How in the hell did it come down to this? Four senators? A brigadier general? I know the explanation Hal gave us why nobody wants to send in the Feds for a raid...."

Bolan also recalled what Brognola told him. "Reading between the lines, we take it out if it's armed. The core of the group will go down fighting. It's up to us. No more casualties of federal agents."

"Deniable expendables, if it blows up in our faces."

"The usual. The senators are a wild card. More than likely they'll throw their hands up to surrender and take their chances."

"Chances? This could turn out to be the worst political nightmare in history when—if—we dump them off to Hal."

"Not our problem."

Bolan stabbed a finger at a point on the satellite imagery of the brigadier general's compound. "Insert me here. You fly in, same deal as when we hit the chem-bio factory. They'll send some guns out to take a look, I'm thinking, and start to push panic buttons, the whole rotten lot running for the front door. This bay window? Put a TOW through it if it looks clear beyond of our senators, then head out front. Take out the motor pool. I'll worry about the senators when I go in. Whether they walk away to spend the rest of their lives in prison, that's up to them."

They stood in silence for long moments and Bolan could easily read his friend's expression. Anger and disappointment showed on Grimaldi's face, making the ace pilot appear as if he were aging before Bolan's eyes. Neither of them could ever fathom how any man, no matter how little or how much power he wielded, could sell out his own country. When he did, he was fair game for the Executioner.

"Let's do it," Bolan told Grimaldi.

THE FOUR SENATORS knew him as Mr. John, but his real name was Andrew Sizemore, and he was a retired NSA black-ops specialist. For days on end now, he had been listening to their squawking under the brigadier general's roof. About their careers. About how they had been abducted and were being held hostage. About how they were faced with ruin and public scandal and prison if they were not let go immediately. So they fretted and paced and paid a lot of attention to the wet bar. Hell, the other three were almost carbon copies of Senator Darren Sterling, he thought.

They weren't allowed to make phone calls or watch television. They were constantly under scrutiny by the eighteen guards inside and outside the mansion, all of them lugging MP-5s and looking hopeful to get the chance to use them on somebody, anybody.

If it was up to Sizemore, he'd just as soon waste the four of them with the Uzi he had slung around his own shoulder. Who was going to miss four more politicians, anyway?

They were gathered once again on one of the two couches, facing each other across the coffee table, working on various cocktails, wringing their hands.

"This is insane," Senator Childs, the latest addition to the group, grumbled. "If you had intended all along to use us as political pawns in whatever your scheme, surely you know that abducting us, holding us prisoner, is certain to bring all of our, uh, indiscretions and whatever your schemes to use us, out into the public light."

"In other words," Senator Sibert growled, "we're all finished, because you got nervous after the situation in Oklahoma, then what the North Koreans did to our people in the Pacific."

"Enough!"

Brigadier General Martin had just stepped from a partitioned cubbyhole deep in the corner of the living room where he'd been trying to have a private conversation with some party unknown. He was dressed in a black turtleneck, khakis and combat boots. A Glock .45 rode in a shoulder holster and a Colt Commando assault rifle hung around his shoulder. Dressed, Sizemore thought, as if he was ready for combat. The past few days, Sizemore had noticed the change in the man. He no longer appeared arrogant, in charge of the moment.

Instead, Sizemore found him lapsing into brooding silence, remaining holed up in his command center down the hall, sometimes for hours, while Sizemore sat out there and played nursemaid to the senators. At the moment, there was a strange and distant stare in Martin's eyes. Sizemore felt the look raising the hairs on the back of his neck.

"We are finished, or at least the four of you are."

"What the hell are you saying?" Senator Sterling whined. "You've extorted us, threatened us with ruin and now what? You're going to go public with what you have on us?"

"Let me be perfectly clear. Certain situations have developed which call for my immediate departure from the country, with, of course, my trusted soldiers here. It seems our friends in North Korea have failed us."

It was the first time in hours Sizemore had noticed Kim of North Korea standing in the corner near the kitchen, watching the senators as if his inscrutable mask was meant to make them more agitated.

Kim was the first to get shot. It came without warning, the Glock out and booming, the hollowpoint round coring between his eyes, snapping his head back and kicking him off his feet. The senators were leaping off the couches, Sizemore hearing their brief screams and pleas as Martin turned the Glock on them.

"What are you doing?"

"No!"

"Are you insane?"

"You can't just kill us!"

All the wailing and gnashing of teeth was washed

away next as Martin pumped out one round after the other into their heads. When the last one flopped to add to the boneless mass sprawled across their couches, Sizemore slowly turned to look at Martin.

"What, Mr. John? They were our meal ticket? They might have been, had things gone according to plan. Once the others of the council vanished with Chongjin, once I received word that Chongjin had gone for himself and in so doing our commander in chief ordered the Haeju installation wiped off the map... News to you? I had to get this from a source deep inside the NSA who thinks he's being followed by the Justice Department. It seems this attack against the North Koreans was an astonishing success, and somehow kept buried, even from me. Seems the press has heard rumors that North Korea was attacked, that the American hostages were freed and are being debriefed and ready to be flown back to States. The President is ready to answer questions about this attack within the hour."

"Now what?"

"We leave the country. All of us. I'll decide where we go once we're in the air."

Sizemore couldn't find his voice for a moment, aware he was looking at a madman right then. He was wondering why Martin was just standing there, staring past him at the dead senators, thinking he needed a few more details about their sudden departure from the country when Martin's tac radio started squawking. Sizemore heard about a gunship coming in from the west. He heard about how they had problems, and in the next moment he was positive their own world was going to hell.

Out back, Sizemore heard the small-arms fire first, voices raised in panic. Then he heard a relentless thunder cutting through, then drowning out the smaller chatter of their subguns. That gunship was unleashing minigun fire.

"Sizemore! Get out there and get the situation under control!"

He almost laughed at that, but he knew if he disobeyed he'd be shot where he stood. Either way, he suspected he was a dead man. Hell, they were all dead men.

An army of black-ops killers, he believed, had come to burn them all down. The least he could do, he figured, was die on his feet.

FORTRESS MARTIN WAS an ivy-and-vine-covered two-story stone mass. Shrubbery and azaleas and hedges appeared to ring the entire building. It was as if the traitor inside was looking to camouflage the place or his sins, but there was no hiding any longer what and where he was.

Bolan chose the wooded hills due northwest of the back of the estate as his insertion point. It was a mere fifty-yard jaunt to hit the back door and blast his way in. Bolan ran as Grimaldi streaked the gunship toward the hardforce bursting out the back door. Grimaldi hit the beam and framed them in a searchlight as they opened fire on the death bird. Men screamed in panic now, blinded by the light.

Bolan counted eight shooters, all of them cutting loose with wild subgun fire, a wing and a prayer from where they stood. Grimaldi scythed them apart like human balloons filled with red dye with a strafing of 7.62 mm rounds.

Bolan closed the gap quickly, M-16 up and searching for fresh targets.

"Striker, I've got two more hostiles ready to come out the back door."

"Hit the front, G-man, take out the motor pool. I'll drive them your way."

And Grimaldi was lifting off, up and away, soaring over the roof.

They took up positions on either side of the doorway, and Bolan didn't give them a second to get it in gear. The 40 mm missile was sailing on for lethal impact, and Bolan was on his way in, set to burst inside after the explosion cleared the path.

SIZEMORE WAS BLOWN off his feet by the explosion that shredded the back door and sent two hardmen flying across the den. He almost lost consciousness, stretched out on his back, but fought to bring himself back to the land of the living before it was too late. His ears were ringing, his eyes trying to focus on something, anything. All he knew was that a goddamn army had them surrounded, hemmed in and marked for extinction.

He couldn't believe he was going to die this way, not after everything he had done on behalf of the Phoenix Council. From driving the final nail of the North Korean sex-extortion angle into the senators, to deliveries of cash, to tapping phones...

He told himself he'd better get it together in a hurry.

He was clearing out the cobwebs, his vision coming back into focus when he saw a tall, dark shadow sweeping through the smoke of the blast. For some reason he waited a moment, certain a full squad of shooters would follow. He couldn't believe it. One guy was rolling his way, all business, all death in his eyes.

He heard himself chuckle, then asked, "So where's the army, pal?"

"You're looking at it."

Sizemore was lifting his Uzi, but the man squeezed the trigger. Nothing but a muzzle-flash and bullets tearing into him, feeling a brief instant of hot pain.

Then nothing at all.

BOLAN RECOGNIZED the four AWOL senators from the Farm's intel package. Obviously they had outlived their usefulness to somebody.

And that somebody was either a bloody mass left behind in the den or running with the pack for the front doors.

Bolan keyed his com-link. "G-man, they did the senators already. They're heading for the front doors. TOW them now!"

The soldier fell back into the den, going for deeper cover. When the blast came, it felt as if the whole house would fall on his head, his senses cleaved apart by the thunder, the floor feeling as if it would break apart and swallow him whole.

The Executioner stepped around the corner, choking on the smoke for a moment. He peered into the great billow of smoke roiling over the mounds of debris where the TOW had blown away the doors and taken out half of the front of the house.

If there were any survivors in those ruins, beneath the drifting palls of smoke, Bolan would be amazed. He tried to tally up the numbers he'd seen running for the doors, but gave it up.

Bodies, or what was left of them, had been blown and smeared all over the foyer and the living room.

The Executioner would give the entire house a walk-through just the same, but he listened to the silence beyond the rotor wash of the gunship.

He could sense nothing but the utter stillness of death.

"THANKS for coming."

"No sweat."

Bolan saw his old friend sitting on the same bench he'd found him when he'd first taken the assignment. How many days since? How many dead since? How much fallout and flak would the Justice Department, the White House get hit with?

The soldier crossed the final few steps at the edge of the Mall. Brognola looked as if he'd aged twenty years since the whole bloody campaign started, his stare wandering over the early-morning crowd of joggers, bicyclists, in-line skaters and sight-seers, the big Fed seeing but not seeing. He looked to Bolan like a man burdened with ghosts, past, present and future.

"I guess Grimaldi needed his beauty sleep? Can't say

I blame him. I'm amazed you could get out of bed yourself."

Bolan looked at the weary grin on Brognola's face and settled on the bench next to him. "Well, I managed a few winks while Jack drove me back and forth over the Pacific."

"I only have a few minutes, then I've got to begin to sort through this whole mess. There are pieces still hanging. Two top counterintelligence operatives from the DIA took the easy way out last night. So did another hotshot general in cahoots with Martin. We're hunting down the last few stragglers on the fringes our late Tolley gave us. Well, it's a mess. I only hope the press doesn't eat the Man alive. You know how those people are. They want to know everything, even in advance, even when it regards national security. Like somebody's jealously guarding the secrets of the universe or hiding the Holy Grail under their bed or some such."

"He made the right call. Whether it gets read by them as all an eye for an eye or not...well, in a big way, it was. It had to be, considering what happened on our own soil."

The big Fed nodded. "I guess it goes without saying, but I'll say it anyway. I'm damn glad you and Jack made it."

Bolan smiled and nodded.

They sat in silence. It was good to sit still and savor a moment of peace, the soldier thought, even if he would never know peace of mind.

Tomorrow would bring another Chongjin, another rat

traitor out of the shadows. Right now it was enough to share a few quiet minutes with his old friend before duty called him once again back to his War Everlasting.

It was good enough.

And in his world, Bolan figured, it probably didn't get any better than this.

Take
2 explosive books
plus a
mystery bonus
FREE

THE Destroyer™

FATHER TO SON

As the long road to the rank of Reigning Master of the venerable house of assassins nears its end, the *Time of Succession* ritual begins. But there is a storm cloud on the horizon of Chiun's retirement and Remo's promotion: a dark nemesis has been reborn from the fires of evil and has unleashed his plot for vengeance. He won't stop until he has fulfilled a prophecy of doom that even Chiun may not be able to thwart: the death of the Destroyer.

Available in October 2002 at your favorite retail outlet.

James Axler
Outlanders®

FAR EMPIRE

Waging a covert war that ranges from a subterranean complex in the desert to a forgotten colony on the moon, former magistrate Kane, brother-in-arms Grant and archivist-turned-warrior Brigid Baptiste find themselves pawns in a stunning strategy of evil. A beautiful hybrid carries an unborn child—a blueprint for hope in a dark world. She seeks Kane's help, unwittingly leading them into a trap from which there may be no escape....

In the Outlands, the shocking truth is humanity's last hope.

DEATH LANDS®

Destiny's Truth

JAMES AXLER

DEATH LANDS

Destiny's Truth

*Available in
December 2002
at your favorite retail outlet.*

Emerging from a gateway in New England, Ryan Cawdor and his band of wayfaring survivalists ally themselves with a group of women warriors who join their quest to locate the Illuminated Ones, a mysterious pre-dark sect who may possess secret knowledge of Deathlands. Yet their pursuit becomes treacherous, for their quarry has unleashed a deadly plague in a twisted plot to cleanse the earth. As Ryan's group falls victim, time is running out—for the intrepid survivors…and for humanity itself.